ACTS OF SUCCESSION

A novel by J. S. Anjum

J.S. Anjum

Acknowledgements

I would like to thank my wife Sahar for her support and encouragement in writing this book and for giving me time to do so. I would also like to thank my friend and colleague DR. William Anapoell. He provided the spark to go after this creative process and has been a great sounding board in this journey.

Table of Contents

1

No one likes hearing "I told you so." Especially if that person is yourself. I told myself security work would be a lucrative business, and all I needed was somebody to run with my idea and put it into play. It was all laid out. I had what I thought to be a reliable investor and a go-to man to do the day-to-day. But, as with most of my other projects, it fell to pieces. I told myself it all hangs on finding the right person to run it, and if I didn't have that, it wasn't going to work. Sure enough, it didn't work. My mounting frustration was overwhelming. Regretfully, I decided to come home to regroup.

Moving back in with one's parents when you're thirty is less than ideal, to say the least. I've been in Las Vegas most of my life and being back for the last six months had not been going well. Don't get me wrong, Vegas is great. I just wish I had come home on my own terms. Being home with my parents doesn't lead to a constructive dialogue. It mostly consists of me being told what to do and how I need to be more responsible. I listen politely, as I've done for years, nod agreeingly to their points, and wait out the rant. In my mind, all I can do is yell out and curse my last business venture for not working, and for now, having to sit through this lecture. If I wasn't reliant on needing a place to stay, I would love to just walk out.

At the end of the current lecture, I found myself needing to go out for a drink and a smoke to alleviate the tension building in my upper neck that was leading to a headache. Luckily, I stumbled upon Sigaros. I heard about it at the Big Smoke Cigar convention that happens every year in Vegas. I swear they have a convention for everything here. I had gone to the convention with a group of my old security buddies from when I worked in Phoenix as a bouncer and head of security for some of the bars. The guys talked up the place so much I decided to check it out.

I went into Sigaros and sat down at the large wooden bar. I didn't plan on staying for long. Just a drink, and maybe I'd pick up a cigar on the way out and go for a walk. From behind the bar, an imposing man of Mediterranean complexion, advanced in his age but not old, walked over.

The man respectfully looked me in the eyes and, in a dry welcoming voice, said, "Name's Sal. What'll you have?"

I stood to meet the man's welcomed tone and gaze. "Name's Leonard. Gin and soda with a lime, please," I said and sat back down.

Now I've been told by some, mostly my family, that my appearance can come off as intimidating given my size, beard, and long hair. I don't disagree that it could be taken that way. That is until people get to know me. Then they find that I am a consummate man of leisure who's up for a good time. It has come in handy to be six three and a fit two hundred fifty pounds. I didn't even have to work out to get this way. It just kind of happened. But the beard and hair, those are my choices. Given my part Irish background, I have a dark-reddish beard and brown straight hair down past my shoulder in a ponytail. The light tan complexion I got from my father. Overall, I think I look awesome.

The way Sal approached me made me want to be in this man's good graces. The simple act of directness in his few words, tone, and eye contact made you feel no judgment, only that of respect and the ask of it in return.

He poured the gin with a heavy, calculated hand. From the look of them, they seemed as though they'd seen a few rough fights. It was interesting. After working in security, you notice different things about people's appearance and how they carry themselves. Sal's presence filled the room. It wasn't intrusive, but the way he walked at his own pace behind the bar and looked up surveying the place was more like that of a bear looking over his terrain to ensure everything was calm and that his customers sund staff were all looked after. The other thing that caught my attention was that even though his knuckles were roughed up, he had not one scar or disfigurement to his face. He was not one to be messed with.

"Gin, eh? You looked like more of a whiskey or bourbon fella," said Sal.

"Nope. Just gin. It's a versatile drink, tastes good, it's lower in calories so I can drink more of it, doesn't give me a hangover, and for some ... it's a super drink."

Sal stopped his almost automated cleaning of glasses that most barman do and paused and looked at me quizzically. "Super drink? What's your basis for that?"

"Gin is made from the juniper berry," I said straight-faced. Junipers are considered a superfood. Therefore," I said with a wide grin, "gin is a superfood."

Sal went back to cleaning his glass and asked with a grin, "So does that line work with the ladies at all?"

"Surprisingly, more often than you'd think," I said as I took a long sip with a deep sigh at the end of it. I closed my eyes for a few moments. It felt good to take a moment and pause. The weight of coming home, the uncertain nature for my future, the lack of prospects of any new venture, the constant nagging from my family were all piling on. But this drink in this moment was cool, refreshing, and made those worries slip away.

Sal looked up now with sharper eyes, as if he knew the weight I felt. "Look over at the walk-in humidor. Try the Partagas Clasico. Matches and cutter are on the bar," and he casually walked away to the end of the mahogany bar. I turned in my high-backed padded wooden bar stool to survey the rest of the place and found the expansive walk-in humidor welcoming me with its floor-to-ceiling shelves of cigars.

At the exact moment I was going to get up to go to the humidor, a group of guys walked in. A beanpole-looking group of five, just barely twenty-one. They were young enough, and I'd seen this night working in bars to play out poorly as the partying went on. A slender, pretty young waitress walked by with drinks in hand, and the group, unassumingly, encircled her. I sat back down in my chair. As young men do, they began to boast and regal stories of their exploits.

"That's nice fellas, take a seat and I'll be with you as soon as I get these drinks to the other customers," she said, trying to politely get herself out of the circle.

The taller one in the group, that I can only say was the leader of the little clan, started to protest. "Come on. We just want to chat. We just got into town. We know you're busy but make time for us. It's Vegas. We're all here to have a good time."

I can't stand when people pull that line or "What happens in Vegas stays in Vegas." No, it doesn't. It goes with you. Everything from photos to the police report to the STD you picked up will go with you.

"You know what happens in Vegas stays in Vegas?" said the taller young man as he slid his arm around her waist, trying to approach her backside. My pulse quickened, and my anger started to boil.

The young waitress was squirming under his touch and was visibly sickened. With a loud voice, she said, "Stop, leave me alone!"

The group of men just laughed. She looked around and saw there was no assistance from her fellow servers in sight, and looked scared. At that moment, I didn't care if I got kicked out of the bar or not. Being an asshole demands a lesson, and these guys needed a little life lesson.

I took a brief sip of my drink. Then I stood up to my full height, tightened my ponytail, and walked over to the group.

"You okay?" I asked the young lady.

She looked up and was visibly shaken but didn't expect to see me. She shook her head no with a scared gaze.

"Hey, we're all having a good time here, buddy," said the young man without turning to look at me. With a dismissive wave of his hand, he said, "Go back to your drink."

The other young men in his group who could see me tapped their friend on the shoulder to look around. The leader of their little ensemble could not have been more than five feet nine inches. It took a moment. He looked me up and down and scoffed. All I wanted to do was punch this guy, but it wasn't my place, and I was hoping to come back here someday, so I refrained.

"What do you think you gonna do? There's five of us and one of you ... with a ponytail," he said smirkingly, his little entourage giggling in the background.

Stepping closer and looking down at him, I thought to myself, *Besides having a drink, I think a fight might be the next most relaxing thing I could do tonight.* I relaxed my shoulders, took a deep breath, and pulled out the hair tie holding my ponytail. I politely grinned at the young man and said, "What ponytail?" The other young men in his group took a step back. The little leader stood ready, but then as I shifted my weight to get a better stance for the oncoming fight, he stopped abruptly.

I heard a deep voice from behind me say, "Leave now and don't come back." It was followed by a menacing steely tone that sent a chill up my spine and that I don't think I could reproduce if I wanted to... "Or else."

Sal walked from behind me after the five young men slowly backed out of Sigaros and approached the young waitress. With great kindness like that of a doting grandfather, he asked, "Are you okay?"

She shook her head "Yes" but was trembling.

You're taking a break," he said to her and took the drinks from the young lady and guided her to what I assumed was the back office, and shut the door to give her some privacy.

I went back to the bar and sat down. Sal casually walked over with the drinks he took from the pretty young waitress and handed them to the customers who were eagerly awaiting their beverages after the little show. He laughed and smiled with them and smoothed over any delay with what can only be described as an effortless charm. Then walked in and out of the large walk-in humidor.

He walked back over behind the large bar to where I was drinking and placed the Partagas Classico in front of me. I took the last pull of my drink, expecting to be asked to leave.

"You a bourbon guy?" I asked.

"Yes, I am."

"Why bourbon?" I asked, hoping I was defusing any anger. Not that I could tell he was angry.

He calmly looked at me again in the eye as he did when I walked into the place and said, "Because it has character."

He looked away and went back to cleaning up the bar. "You looking for work?" he said. My eyes were a little wide with astonishment. I had half expected to be asked to leave after confronting another patron. Believe me, if Sal had asked me to go, I would not have hesitated to politely leave.

Sal continued. "I expect a certain clientele in my establishment. I believe you'd be able to ensure Sigaros remains a classy place. Come in tomorrow at six in the evening, and I'll give you a rundown of how things are to be handled," and he casually walked away. As he did, he followed up with a slight turn of his head and a pause in his step. "Wear a suit for work. Tie is up to you."

I looked to both sides of me, exasperated. What just happened? How did I just get a job offer? Do I want to do this? I don't want to be a bar guy. I want to be an entrepreneur, and I have so many good ideas. That being said, it has been six months since any income, and I was running short on funds and patience at being home.

From the end of the bar, Sal said in a deep, steely voice that was loud enough for all the people in the bar to hear, "The cigar is on the house, Leo."

2

Six months ago, if you would've told me I'd be working day-to-day security again, I would've called you an idiot. Sal had a way of putting things that made you listen. But more importantly, he puts things in such a way where he forces you to reflect on your own shortcomings. I've seen him do this a few times with friends, staff, and even strangers that he meets for the first time in Sigaros. He's like Yoda—if Yoda was a six feet three-inch older Italian man. I, luckily, had skirted his mind trick. I'd been too busy setting up the improved security system Sal had asked me to help with—which included training the bartenders, staff, and new security personnel on how to deal with difficult situations when they arise. A perk that I just recently picked up in the last month, in what seemed to be my ever-expanding job description, was helping with the cigar distributors.

Sal has an amazing selection of cigars. They were organized by region of origin. The humidor was a good 250 square feet with floor-to-ceiling cigars and a dark marble-topped island in the center. It had that great aroma all walk-in humidors have of deep earthy tobacco combined with the heavy air of humidity. As you passed the different sections of the room, you could pick up notes for each particular region known for its coffee, nuts, herbs, and spices. Each time I'd walk through the door, the smells were so vivid they'd conjured up a memory of a smoke I'd had at different places and times in my life. It was like taking a world trip all in the span of a brief walk around a room.

I strolled into work, looking for my notebook. The place opens at two in the afternoon, and I usually get there just a little after. By the time I arrived, all the staff were already there working like busy little bees. Sal is always here; it really is his home. He's usually in the back going over paperwork before opening. I couldn't find it before I left last night. I kept all my good ideas in that book. One day one of these plans would make it off the page and turn into a lucrative and hopefully cushy project. I had this great new idea in my head when I woke up and needed to write it down. Luckily, I found the notebook next to a new shipment of Padrón and Barrio 1964 edition cigars. I eagerly looked at the boxes and took a deep inhale, and savored the rich aroma. I rubbed my hands together and told myself, "That's how I'll end the night; with one of these."

I said hi to the twins who were restacking the bar and to Sara, who was going over last night's registrar receipts. I posted up to the bar with my notebook in hand and began to jot down my latest epiphany when from the back office, I heard in a booming but not obtrusive voice, "Leonard! I need to see you in my office."

"Sure thing, Sal. I'm just writing down this idea. I've had another great thought for a project. It's based on making the perfect breakfast sandwich. It's gonna be great. Don't tell anyone."

Exasperated and with a deep sigh, Sal said, "Again with the projects." In a decidedly steelier tone, he said, "Good. Great. That's fantastic. Now, Leo! I've got things to do."

Usually, when he has that tone, he's not kidding around. I learned that the hard way the first few days I worked here. Early on, I was testing my boundaries with him to see how far I could get. I figured at any new job, you have to know who you're working for, and testing to see how far people will let you go is a good starting point. It was later in the evening on a not-so-busy night, and the last distributor for the day had come and gone. I was sitting at the bar having a delightful Romeo y Julieta cigar when I heard a noticeable commotion from what sounded like the establishment next door.

Sigaros was tucked away from the Las Vegas Strip in a nice little plaza cul-de-sac along with two restaurants and a coffeehouse on one side, and on the opposite side were two law offices and a small state bank. Directly next to Sigaros was a steakhouse called Mickey's. It had to have been there as long as Sal's place, nearly thirty years, along with the other businesses. Mickey's was a great steakhouse with nice dark lighting and vintage booths and had that old-time charm and ambiance. The martinis were a little too strong for my taste but a good spot to take a date all the same. Given that the ruckus was not affecting Sigaros, I paid no attention to the developing argument that I could hear building up outside. All the patrons were starting to notice, though.

It got so loud that Sal stepped out of his office and calmly said to me. "Leo, go check it out."

I turned in that most comfortable of high-backed barstools and quizzically said, "It's next door, boss. Not our problem."

The look in Sal's eyes was one of disappointment and, without pause, he headed purposefully to the door with an assured fortitude in his brow, and with his back turned to me, told me stiffly, "Follow me."

I threw my hands up in the air with a slap on my thighs and a shake of my head. This is why people need to mind their own business. Trouble happens when you open other people's doors. I had seen it time and time again in the bars that I worked at, and I'd gotten into my share of scuffs regarding others' problems.

I had to quicken my pace behind Sal. He was surprisingly fast for a man that I thought was in his late sixties. I had asked him once how old he was, and all he told me was "Old enough." I even tried to push him on it to find out his birthday, and all he told me was that he was too mature to have a birthday anymore. I let him see me roll my eyes when he answered me on that question. To my surprise, it was followed by a chuckle that I did not expect to hear.

As we approached Mickey's front door, we saw the owner Gino engaged in a protesting argument with a customer. Gino couldn't have been more than five feet tall, was not trim but still carried himself well, had a full salt and pepper head of hair, a full beard, and a decidedly Roman nose. Apparently, the final customer of the evening wanted to drive himself home. Gino was not going to let that happen. There is such a thing as a dram shop law where the bartender, and in effect, the restaurant owner, is responsible for the patron who drank at their establishment and decides to then drive home intoxicated. Gino was adamantly petitioning the middle-aged man to wait for a cab that he had called for him. The patron was becoming impatient and, with keys in hand, kept motioning to his car. When the middle-aged man saw Sal and I, he stopped abruptly.

With a sigh of relief, Gino said, "See, it's here. I want you to get home safe. We'll get your car back to you tomorrow. One of my guys will see to it."

The man hazily looked at Gino and hugged him, followed by a slur of words and, "Thanks for always looking out for me." He got into the cab and Gino leaned in and gave him the address of the man's home.

Gino turned to Sal and me. "Thanks, fellas, I had it."

"I know you did," said Sal. "I just wanted to see you in action … it's been so long." He chuckled with a grin.

With a smirk, Gino spoke. "Keep laughing, Sal. How much money did I take from you in that last poker game?"

Sal dismissively waved his hand. "See you at the next poker night?"

"Absolutely," said Gino with a wide grin. "I love taking your money. Bueno Sera."

"Fino alla prossima volta,"said Sal.

As this went on, I stood ready and still behind Sal in case something went south. Sal waited until Gino got back into his restaurant. Sal stood still and motionless for a moment. It was just him and I outside in the cool November evening Vegas finally has to offer. The weight of the moment was heavy. I was about to turn to go back in when Sal spoke in that same tone when I first met him in the altercation with those beanpole kids that sent a chill up my spine.

"I expect you to follow my requests. I will not ask more of you than I expect you can handle."

"Come on. Really? You're upset that I didn't go and look at another place's problem?" I said.

"Yes," Sal said and turned to meet my gaze with a hard look. "How strong do you think I am?

"What?" I said, surprised.

"How strong do you think I am and why?" he asked calmly and with a look that was not going to accept anything but an honest answer.

"You're damn strong and not one to mess with," I said with my hands raised in question. "Why? I don't know." *What was he looking for?* I asked myself.

"Alone, I'm weak," he said with that same steel in his voice and shook his head. "True strength comes from the friends and community I surround myself with. If I or those around me are not able to help in times of need, I would never be where I am now. You help others, Leo. Doing the right thing is hard, but it begs to be done. Gino and I were strangers when we first met. He and I started our places around the same time. In a community, you look out for each other and have each other's back. It's not just the place you work. It's where you are and what surrounds you that needs safeguarding. Next time I ask you to go look at what's going on, I expect you to do so. If you don't feel you're up to that task, leave."

Sal walked past me into the bar. I stood there looking out at the blinking neon signs on the Strip. For as tall as I was, I felt smaller than Gino right now. I bowed my head and took a breath, turned, and went back into the bar. The old man had a point.

That being said, this time, when he asked me in that same tone, I shut my book and begrudgingly looked up to the ceiling saying to myself, *If I only had a little more time to perfect my ideas, I would be on easy street.* I stood and buttoned my suit jacket and walked to Sal's office.

3

"All right, you calm down, old man. Don't get all uppity. I'm coming," I said with notebook in hand, strolling toward Sal's office. I gave a quick rap on the door and entered.

To call it an office is understating its grandeur. It was more of an office meets an old school den. It was a large dark mahogany walled space lined with shelving running just off the ceiling of all four walls crammed with books, paintings, and old photos of Sal and all his friends and acquaintances from over the years. Some I could recognize as major celebrities or local ones, but there were so many that I had no clue who they were. There must have been photos going back to when Sal started the place. A minibar on the right—although "minibar" understates the high-quality liquor stored within. A 40-inch TV over a brick fireplace you could walk into, and planted squarely in front of it was a deep leather couch draped with the softest blankets you'd ever felt. In the left corner stood a five-person poker table with last night's cigar butts and half-spent drinks emptied by the regular Monday night poker players. Mostly the participants were Sal's friends from old Vegas who were still around, which included Gino next door.

The centerpiece of the room was the massive wooden desk that held Sal's laptop, mounds of paper, and the ever-present bottle of Blanton's single-barrel bourbon whiskey. He was only ever gone on Sunday to church until midafternoon and took the occasional Tuesday off to nurse any possible hangover that occurred from Monday night's games. Monday and Tuesday were the only nights we closed early.

Sal was standing at his desk with his back to me, filing away paperwork. He is especially tall for an older Italian guy, maybe a hair taller than me. He had a full head of silver hair speckled with a few black strands. You'd think he was more Irish than Italian. He's not slouched over like how some people get with age. He always stands straight, like he had a rod down his back. You could tell when he was younger, he was well muscled. Not a bodybuilder but one of those guys who had that farm-boy strength. He always wore a buttoned-down collared shirt and dress slacks with suspenders. And he never went anywhere without his fedora and a jacket.

He looked like he just stepped out of the 1950s or 1960s, and I have a feeling that's when he was in his prime. Although I think if he ever heard me say it, he'd show me what he could do now and make me wish I'd never met him back in the day. He's quick with a joke and can talk to anyone and everyone. With those he liked, he laughed loudly and as often as possible, with all his lung power behind him, and never ever treated anyone with disrespect ... unless they had it coming.

I think I was one of the only ones who talked to Sal that way, but I think he kind of liked it. He never told me otherwise. I get away with a lot of stuff because of my general awesomeness.

With my hands at my side in a superman pose and a smile, I said, "All right, what ya need, boss?"

Never turning around, Sal continued to speak in an even tone. "How do you like it here?"

My hands dropped, and with a furrowed brow, I stated, "I like it here. Wait ... are you firing me?"

I was a little worried because there may or may not have been a little incident that happened last Tuesday, and I hadn't heard anything from Sal about it. I may have overstepped my role as Sigaros' cigar buyer, house connoisseur, and security lead.

"If it's because of that one customer last Tuesday, listen, he was a prick and needed to be thrown out. He was rude, condescending, and insulting to the patrons and staff. More importantly, he made fun of my ponytail."

Now facing me with a grin on his face, Sal said, "Well, it wasn't so funny when you lifted him up by his throat."

I politely stepped forward to the desk now that Sal finally cracked a smile and, in a dutiful tone, said, "I wanted to remind him in a way that he would remember how a man should act and to treat people with respect."

Sal then sat in his large, leathered, and age-worn office chair and motioned for me to sit across from him in his equally age-worn guest chair. With relaxed shoulders and steepled hands, he followed up. "And then threw him out on what was left of his pride? The twins and Sara were working that night, and they told me the next day."

With a wave of my hand, I sat back in the chair and said, "Well, I'm just saying I don't think I should be fired for that."

Sal raised a quick hand with his palms up. "Stop. I'm not firing you. You're right. He was a prick. If I was here, I would've thrown him out myself. I don't stand for that kind of nonsense."

My shoulders relaxed. "Phew, that's a relief. You were getting that serious tone in your voice with the 'Now, Leo!' comment." I straightened up in the chair. "What do you need to talk about then?"

Sal leaned over the desk and grabbed his glass. "I'm glad you stand your ground and know when to act, kid." He motioned to the minibar with his free hand and took a sip on his drink. "Get yourself a drink and sit down."

Still testing to see how far I could push the old man, I made a line for the bottle on his desk while he moved to the couch. Just as he sat, he saw I wasn't at the bar.

With a double take and a quick response, Sal protested, "And not my bourbon, ya savage! Anything else from the bar over there that you want," pointing back to the minibar.

With a grin and hands raised, I said, "All right, all right. No need to get all worked up. Just keeping you on your toes, old man." I walked over to the bar and yelled back, "I'm taking some Bluecoat, and calm down with the name-calling."

Again, I heard him say "Savage," but this time, I could tell he said it with a grin. Sal couldn't stand gin. I have a feeling gin and he had a disagreement some years back, and they just haven't spoken since. I drink it because a good gin cocktail is like the sweet nectar of the gods. Never have a gin martini shaken; it waters down the alcohol when you do that. I never understood why in all those films, Bond basically drank watered-down drinks. It really takes away from the experience of a good gin martini. I'm plus-minus on the olives.

I made myself my cocktail and sat on the couch next to Sal.

"For the last five months, you've done great at shaping up the cigar lounge: improving security, helping with the distributors, even advertising, and bringing in clientele. This place was doing ... quite well before, but now it seems everyone in Vegas knows about the joint."

Like a kid who got an "A" in an exam, I smiled and said, "I'm kind of impressed too. I'm surprised you didn't advertise like this before. You could've been more well-known years ago and been making a killing."

A nod of his head in agreement. "Ah, well, that was never my angle. I always liked how old Vegas felt, with local joints you could only know about by word of mouth." A deep sigh. "But like everything else, with time, things must change. I think time's up." As he slapped his thigh, "Things will have to change."

With a raised eyebrow, I said, "Don't get all sentimental, old man. Things always change. Hell, we've both seen how this city has changed over the years. You more than me. You've been in Vegas forever. You've made it this long in town without a hitch. You know how to read the city."

With a decidedly more serious tone, Sal spoke. "That's why I need to talk to you. I want you to take a run at managing this place. You know how to make a good deal with the distributors and when to stick it to them when they try and overcharge. The staff here respects you, and well, you remind me a little of myself when I started this place. I want you to take on more. I need someone to look out for Sigaros."

"I'm not sure, Sal. I told you before I wasn't planning on being here longer than the six months. I have a lot of ideas I'm working on that just need a little tweaking, and I'll be off on my own. I just don't see myself as a bar guy or a cigar manager. I've always seen myself inventing something or having my own place or—"

Holding his hand up, Sal broke in and put his drink down on the wooden ring-stained table in front of us. "Hold on, Leo. Let me stop you." He leaned in. "I'm good at reading people. I know you. You're rebellious, smart, and a personable guy. You use your experience guided by intelligence to lead you, but you don't finish what you start. You need to take responsibility." He paused and took a long sip on his cocktail. "I was a bit like that, and something happened that forced me to change for the better. I want to give you an opportunity to change."

"I don't know, Sal. I really appreciate the offer. I-I'd need to think about it and work out the kinks."

Leaning back in that deep couch, he said, "Let me put it to ya this way. Don't think of yourself as a lounge guy or cigar manager. Think of yourself as an entrepreneur, with this being a means to an end to get those other ideas of yours off and running. It's a good offer, Leo. Think it over."

The ice cubes in my drink clinked around like little bells, and I looked down into the glass. "Hey, you sick or going someplace, old man?"

"Hell, no!" he said, half spilling his drink. "I might be old, but I'm still good enough to take you down, kid," he said with a grin. "Sigaros and Vegas are my life. I'd never leave either. Too much history ... good ... and bad."

I held my hands up in an attempt to withdraw my previous comment. "Okay, Sal. Just checking."

"Don't get any ideas like I'm leaving this place to you or making you partner or something ... you're good but not that good. I need someone with a head on his shoulders and the common sense to follow through with what needs to be done. I'd like to think you have the makings of that guy."

I thought back to that meeting of ours a few months back when I first started. He knew I had hesitations working at a bar, but then he said something that resonated with me that I won't forget. "A person who never made a mistake never tried anything new. Go after your passions boldly, and you will find unexpected forces aiding your cause."

We both took a long gulp of our respective drinks. This time I spoke first. "If, that's if I say yes, I would have to have allotted time to work on my other project. I would want to try and run the place my way. Advertise how I like, expand the place, kick out people who, shall we say, need a lesson in manners, and bring in a little of my own flair. Oh, and! We need to upgrade the alarm system here and add a few cameras."

I saw a gentle glow in Sal's face, and the beginnings of a smile started to grow. "As long as this place never loses the personal touch and class that Vegas was built on, you have a deal." He stuck out his scarred hand and looked me in the eye. I met his gaze assuredly and firmly shook it.

With a grin, I said, "Then what are we waiting for? Go tell the rest of the guys that I'm their new boss."

Sal laughed loud and heartily. He hadn't done that all morning. "You're not the boss. I'm the boss. You're just in charge when I'm not here, is all. Got it." And winked. "Continue to use that experience guided by intelligence."

"Got it, boss," I said with a smile. "All right, all right, well, go tell the rest of the guys here that I'm in charge when you're not around."

He smiled wide and laughed again. "I told them last week after you threw that guy out."

"Are you serious?" I said with an astonished look on my face.

I laughed with Sal this time. I like the idea of this as a trial run at being an entrepreneur. Maybe it'll be good for me.

Sal stood. "Leo, I'm going out for the rest of the day." And made for his hat and suit coat.

With a sideways glance, I asked, "Really? You never leave here before ten at night."

After fixing his hat and buttoning his suit, he said, "Well, now that you're here, I can. Keep an eye on the place."

"Will do, Sal."

"Make sure you lock up when you leave." And he headed for the office door.

"Don't I always?" standing and gulping down the last of my drink.

"No, no, you don't."

"Yeah, yeah. I've got it," waving my hands again in dismissal.

This time he stopped and looked over his shoulder and, in a caring tone that I was surprised to hear, said, "I know you do, Leonard. I trust you to take care of things. Good luck, kid."

4

I walked out of the office a little taller than I'd gone in. I paused and surveyed the rest of Sigaros. It looked different somehow. Not that anything dramatic in its appearance happened in the last twenty minutes. It felt brighter and bigger in some way.

When you walk into Sigaros from the heat of Las Vegas, you notice the cool, humid moisture in the air as an almost tropical breeze hits you, immediately giving your skin a reprieve from the dryness of the desert. There's a dull rhythm of jazz being played overhead. Sigaros is divided into a few sections. In front of you is an open space with bistro-styled tables of two and four seats with small yellow-lit table lamps. Each table is separated by short tropical plants to provide privacy. Black leather booths line each side with more cushioned low-backed leather and wooden chairs. From the open space at the entrance, you pass two dark massive wooden pillars that light up the place with their wall-mounted bronzed candelabras that shine a warm glow all over. As you pass the pillars, the bar opens up to a well-worn but well-kept mahogany bar with seating for eight up front and two on each side, along with four extra barstools situated out of sight behind the large pillars. To the left side of the counter are the restrooms and supply room. To the right of the counter is another open space with rich amber-colored leather lounge chairs and small wooden side tables with ashtrays that form their own encirclement of the walk-in humidor.

You'd think the smell of the cigars would overwhelm the place, but Sal had installed a large vent and air purification system that would rival any of today's casinos to filter out any smell a customer might take offense to. Instead, the air was clean and refreshing. Sal's office was just behind the bar facing the humidor.

Sal kept the place to a bare-bones operation. It consisted of the bartender, Sara, a barback named Mike, and the twins Mia and Kate, who waited the tables. Sal took on the rest of the tasks from host to barkeep to confidant and sage to the person who cleaned up and took out the trash. No job was too big or small for him.

Mike was still in college over at UNLV and worked mostly Thursday through Sunday nights. He seemed like a hard-working guy. He was maybe just twenty-one, if not a year or so shy, clean-shaven, with a wiry frame and average height, short-cropped blond hair, and thick-rimmed glasses. The twins were nothing alike. Mia was the slender young waitress I met that first day I walked in when those guys were giving her a hard time. She was maybe five foot, blonde, a little shy and soft-spoken, and I think ever since that first night, she may have had a little crush on me. But maybe that's just me overthinking it. Kate was almost five-eight with fiery red hair and a more muscled build. She was self-confident, bold, and didn't take any crap. She had always been grateful to me stepping in to help her sister.

The dark mahogany bar was filled with customers. Sara was running it with what seemed little effort at all. I knew that was hardly the case. She worked hard to make it look easy. She was dressed in a black blouse and tight black jeans. She has short dark-brown shoulder-length unevenly cut hair with a slim frame and deep brown eyes. She wore black platform boots that put her at about five-nine or ten. I've seen more than one patron get tongue-tied from when they first meet her.

The variety of customers were chatting away, laughing with each other, listening intently to their companions, or sitting back leisurely sipping their drink of choice. The one commonality beyond the good time had by all was that each of their glasses was full. The twins were busy serving customers, from the booths to the private tables and lounge chairs. The place was in good form. I saw Sal turn as he exited the front door, tipped his hat, and was gone.

I made my way over to the old mechanical register that was flanked by a more updated credit card machine. *Sal has to get rid of some of this older stuff and update the bar,* I thought to myself. I looked up again and started to see what else needed attention when

Sara bumped her shoulder into my elbow. "Put this bottle of Redbreast back up there, would you?"

I grabbed the bottle and grinned. "Boots not big enough?" and turned and placed the bottle on the highest part of the shelf.

She stared at me and leaned in, pulling on my suit collar. "I could have done it." And with a purr, "The boots are just right." Just as she got close enough for me to smell her jasmine perfume, she abruptly shoved me away, putting me a little more off balance than I had expected, and I stumbled back two steps. "I just like bossing men around, is all," she said with a smirk and went back to tidying up the bar.

"So, where'd Sal go? He never leaves before ten," she asked as she continued to restock the fruits.

With a shrug, I answered, "He didn't say, but…" a large smile across my face as I slowly looked directly at Sara, "he said I'm in charge."

She rolled her eyes at me and made sure none of the patrons nearest her at the bar could see. "Oh, God. Why the hell did he do that?"

I looked at her, a little taken aback and surprised, then said, "Sal said he told you all last week."

"Yeah, I told him not to," she said in a mumbled voice, smiling and looking at the customers.

"Why not?" I said as I turned to her, my feelings a little hurt.

"You're not committed to it," she said plainly.

She went back to picking up the nearest empty drink as a man signaled for another. "Listen, Leo, you're great. You're a nice guy, and you've been here six months. I've been here almost four years while working to get through law school. Between school and working here, I've seen a few people come and go. You know what I can spot a mile away? A person who isn't committed to the task at hand. You don't seem to be the guy who follows through."

It wasn't appealing when I heard it from Sal not twenty minutes ago. It certainly hasn't been fun hearing it from my parents for the last six months and even before that, and it was infuriating to hear it from Sara. She could see me tighten up my fists, my shoulders go straight, and my jaw clench. "Hey!" she said, and this time punched my upper arm with her elbow like a kickboxer. With a hushed strong tone, she said "Prove me wrong. Prove Sal right. Prove it to yourself."

My muscles relaxed a little, and I looked at her, and those big brown eyes stared back. "Not everyone started out knowing where they were going. It's okay. But you have to make a stand and a choice." This time she placed a soft hand on mine. "Get out of your head." She straightened up. "Sal left you in charge," she said now with a slap of the bar towel. "Get to it."

I felt a little more relaxed and was taking in everything she just said. "Still bossing me around, I see," I said, looking over Sigaros with a weak smile.

"Absolutely," she said this time without looking and headed toward the far end of the bar to talk to the barback, Mike. "Plus, the twins look like they need a little help."

I looked over to one of the corners of the place and saw Mia gently waving her hand for me to come over to help one of the customers. I looked back toward Sara, sighed, and made my way over.

5

Being the boss is so tiresome. Between entertaining the customers, troubleshooting issues with supply with Sara and Mike, fixing one of the bathrooms that went on the fritz, and making sure I didn't mess it all up, I felt physically and emotionally spent. The last customer of the night was safely ushered out by Sara. I had sent the twins and Mike home about an hour ago. No sense them staying till two in the morning if it was quieting down. Most places in Las Vegas don't close down. Vegas is a spot that's open all night. There's always something happening and something to do. I can't tell you the number of times I've seen customers hear "Last call" and look down at their watches perplexed. Nobody ever seems to protest when Sal says, "Last call." However, when I said it tonight, I got an audible grumble. Luckily Sarah was there to back me up and ring the bell above the bar near the cashier. All the customers settled up, and I walked Sara out.

I couldn't wait to go home and feel the coolness of a pillow on my head. I turned and looked at Sara. After working in a bar all night, she still looked put together enough to hit the strip, and I think she had the energy to do it.

I let the tiredness show in my voice and said, "Night, Sara. Thanks for all your help tonight. I couldn't have done it without you." I turned to walk away.

Sara grabbed my hand and looked up at me. She held my wrists with both her hands and shook them, saying, "You did... all right tonight. Keep it up." She let go of my wrists, and with a grin, said, "But you're no Sal." She turned and walked away, and I took the opportunity to follow her silhouette to where she parked her car. It was a nice end to the night.

I turned to walk away when I heard from over my shoulder Sara say in a lyrical tone, without turning around, "Leo, lock up." I stopped and hung my head down, turned on my heels, and rummaged through my pockets until I found the key that Sal uses for the deadbolt. I reached up to the door and locked it shut. I swung the keys in my hand like an old western gunfighter and dropped them into my pocket. This time I turned again with the hope that I didn't forget anything and headed to my ride.

I don't live very far away from Sigaros, and with my last venture going belly up, I didn't have much to spend on transportation. What I did have was an old used bike that I slapped an electric motor on. Now you may think it's funny to see a guy of my size in a suit riding down the streets of Vegas on an electric bike. Or even question the safety of riding a bicycle in almost the middle of the night. Two things: one, I was saving a ton of money on gas and insurance, and two, regarding safety, nobody wants a me-sized dent in their car, so I got a wide berth when I was cycling down the streets.

I was starving. I didn't notice it until after locking up. Not too far away from where I live is a glorious little taco shop. I turned on the electric motor, and it hummed to life, and I headed over to Roberto's. This time of night, you'd think would be dead, but this is Vegas. It was hopping. There had to be at least six cars in the drive-through line and another ten people inside. Luckily I've come here enough so that they know me. I leaned the bike up against the glass windowed exterior and walked in. With a ding of the bell above the door, the smaller Hispanic older gentleman behind the cashier looked up. "Leo!" he said with a smile. "Buenos noches, amigo, regular?" It didn't matter what time of day or how busy it was when I walked in, he always greeted me. A few years back, when I was visiting my parents from out of town, a few customers were being a little rude, and I had instructed them to leave. Since then, Miguel and his wife Sophia have always been fans. Sophia ran the kitchen, and Miguel lovingly referred to her as Mama.

I smiled back. "Buenos noches, senor. Mama here?"

Smiling and nodding to the kitchen behind him, he said, "Por supuesto. But of course."

"Then the regular it is," I said, patting my belly.

The burrito took only five minutes, and I was back on my way home. Within fifteen minutes, I pulled my electric bicycle up to the side of the house and plugged it in near the side door. It was a little difficult eating and biking my way home, especially with all the potholes. *I'm surprised I didn't get any food on my suit. Oh, that's a good idea for an invention. A burrito bike rack. I'll write that down in my notebook.* But for now, all I could think of was getting to bed. I fumbled for the keys to the house and quietly entered through the side door.

Like I said earlier, I have been staying at my parents' place, and I make every effort to not make too much noise when I come home after two in the morning. I swear, I think they have sonar-like hearing. Both of them still work. They don't work at any of the casinos or hospitality industries. They work in administration for the hospitals in town and still get up early. Well, at least fairly early for my taste. Going to work by seven in the morning is an ungodly hour. I couldn't stand the idea of getting up in the morning to go to work every day at that time. That's why I want to work on these ideas for my entrepreneurship. If I could just get a good thing going, I could make my own schedule, come and go as I please, and be beholden only to myself. I quietly placed my keys on the counter and headed to the kitchen for a glass of water.

I opened the well-stocked fridge and went for a nice cool pitcher of water. As I went to close the refrigerator door, I almost dropped the ice-cold water all over my suit. To my extreme surprise, my dad was standing right behind the door as I closed it. My dad is about five feet nine inches with salt and pepper hair in a full beard that I had never seen him without. He stood there in his bathrobe, hands in his pockets, staring at me blankly.

"Geeze, Dad. You scared me half to death. Sneeze or cough or shuffle next time," I said as I caught my breath. As he's not usually up at this hour, I looked at him and asked, "Everything okay?"

With a still tone, he said, "You're to help your mother in the morning. Your brother is coming over to help as well. It should only take about an hour of your time. Be up at seven thirty."

In protest, I said, "It's three in the morning. I just got done with work, and I have to work tomorrow. Can we do it on my day off?"

With a sigh and an unwavering look of disapproval, he started in on his lecture. "You need to have a more stable job. Going out and working all hours of the night is not responsible. If you're here under our roof, you will help out when we ask. If you don't like it, you can leave any time." With that, he turned and walked back to the hallway, and I heard him making his way up the stairs to my parents' bedroom.

I tilted my head as far back as it could go and, with a deep sigh, said to myself. "If I could just get one of these projects up and running, I'd be out of here."

I threw my suit jacket and button-down shirt on the kitchen chair, placed my lace-up Oxford shoes near the door, and made my way to my room. My room was at the opposite end of the house upstairs and was far enough away where no one could hear me. I opened the door, changed out of my suit pants into basketball shorts, crashed on top of my comforter, and finally placed my head on that ice-cold pillow I had been so eagerly awaiting. It felt like falling into a cloud, and my eyes shut.

It couldn't have been long that I was down when I awoke to hear, "Goddamn son of a bitch rat bastard!" Sunshine was peeking through my curtains. Oh man, it was already morning. It felt like I'd just laid down. The words I heard were coming from downstairs. I rushed to the staircase and hurried down to where I heard my mother repeat the same phrase. There, standing by the bathroom next to the kitchen, was my mother, hands on hips, with a significant scourer that, for some reason, was pointed in my direction.

In a half-asleep voice that sounded like I swallowed a frog, I said, "Ma! What's wrong? You okay?"

With the scourer, she pointed with a firm arm to the bathroom toilet and said, "Did you do this?"

"What are you talking about?" I said, perplexed, finally finding my voice, and trying to wipe the sleep out of my eyes.

Drawing a step closer to me and pointing her finger up into my face, she let me have it. "How many times do I have to tell you to put the toilet seat down? You're a grown man. You're lucky I'm your mother; otherwise, I'd pull all your chest hairs out one by one." Now with her hands on her hips, she nodded to herself, saying, "Actually! I still might do it if I see this happen again. Got it?!"

Oh man, I do think it was me who left it up before I headed to Sigaros last night. Crap. She's really gonna pull out my chest hairs this time if I own up to it. She's pissed. In a calm, reassuring voice, I lied. "Ma, I'm sorry. I'll talk to Gabriel. He's done this a few times this last week when he was over. I'll remind him." She visibly started to calm down. The redness in her face and ears started to dissipate. I placed my arm around her shoulders and gave her a big squeeze. Looking down at her, I said, "Don't work yourself up so much. You're going to have a coronary."

She looked up at me, squinting her eyes. "Your brother? Really?"

"Yes, Ma. He's been stressed with the architect project he's been working on and was hurrying in and out of here after helping you." I paused and looked at her with as much regret as I could muster that early in the morning and, with puppy dog eyes, said, "He just forgot."

With a deep sigh and now with her hands at her sides, she said, "Fine. He has been stressed with that project. Go get ready. You and Gabe are to help me move all my Christmas decorations from storage."

I stopped and went still. *Oh no, not again*, I thought. Every year she puts out this ornate Christmas village all over the house. It takes

41

ages, and my brother and I hate it. Ma loves it. Dad could care less about it as long as Mom's happy.

"Come on, Ma," I said in protest. "Not this year."

She placed her hands on the sides of my head, pulled me down, and kissed me on my forehead. "Go. Shower. Get ready for the day. Gabe will be here soon." She left to get ready for the upcoming on-slaught of elves, reindeer, Santas, ice rinks, and mini Christmas vil-lages that we were about to assemble. Like a general awaits troop in-spection, she started walking around the house preparing the sites for set up.

I knew there was no winning and loafed back upstairs into the shower and dressed. My brother was downstairs by the time I was done. He's a trim but fit six feet, always clean-shaven, with short brown hair never out of place. He was drinking a cup of coffee at the table, and I joined him.

"You ready for this, Leo?" he asked, finishing the cup.

"Absolutely not," I said, dreading what was about to come.

The next few hours were just as expected. "Move that center-piece. Put Santa's workshop there. I need more snow boys." It was exhausting, and it didn't help that I had barely slept four hours. Gabe and I finally finished at about eleven thirty. I had just enough time to head upstairs, nap for thirty minutes, then shower and get ready to go back to Sigaros.

My brother and I were only a few years apart. He left for college when I was a sophomore in high school. We'd been close but never hung out in the same social scene. He was an architect in town, had a wife, and two awesome kids. My niece and nephew were a blast; tons of energy and lots of fire, but a real good pair of kids. My brother did all right for himself at home and at work. He's guilty of throwing himself into his work. I swear, if I wasn't around to tell him not to work so hard all the time and live a little, he'd be on a job site every day of the week all day long.

"Work going all right?" he asked as I headed upstairs. "You know you're always welcome to come and work with me. I have plenty of stuff I could use you for."

He meant well. He was always trying to look out for me. He never got that I was trying to stand on my own two feet or that one of my ideas was going to take off. I stopped and turned to him a few feet up on the stairs. "No, I'm good. Things at Sigaros are going okay. It's given me a lot of time to work on my ideas for some projects."

He held up his hands in protest. "Got it. I'm glad it's going well. Gotta run and get back to work. I'll see ya." Just before closing the door, he poked his head back around it. "Hey!" I stopped near the top of the staircase. In a quizzical tone, Gabe said, "Any idea what Ma was going on about? She told me it's okay that I forgot this time and said she knew how busy I was. Did I miss an anniversary or something?"

Oh crap, it was about the toilet seat I left up and blamed on him. With as straight a face as I could, I said "No clue," turned, and with wide eyes, hurried up to my room. I closed the door and sighed as I heard Gabriel shut the front door. I looked at the time. Damn, no time for a nap. I headed to the washroom and got ready to go back to Sigaros. At least we close early on Monday.

6

Ring ring… ring ring.

In her boots, Sara gingerly stepped down off the barstool she was using to place the last bottle of Maker's Mark that Mike had brought up from the back storage up on the shelf. As she approached the old handset, she glanced up at the clock above the cash register and yelled out to the twins. "Any bets this is Leo saying he'll be here just after we open?"

"Ten bucks, it's not him," said Mia without looking up as she dusted off her last table.

"Twenty, it is him," Kate said defiantly with a wrinkle in her nose as she slapped her bar towel in Mia's direction.

"Book's closed!" yelled Sara waving her hand horizontally in the air. She picked up the old receiver and notepad. There was a standing rule from Sal to write down all callers and times to make sure Sal could follow up. "Sigaros, this is Sara. Happy hour running daily from 3:00 p.m. to 6:00 p.m. How may I help you?"

A strong but raspy voice of a man answered back. "I'd like to talk to my good friend Sal. Tell him it's an old friend."

Not the first time someone had called with that opening line. With a shrug, Sara replied, "Sure. Hold the line." She jotted down the time and labeled it 'Old friend called to speak with my good friend Sal.' Covering the phone, she glanced at the twin saying, "Not him." The twins simultaneously stuck their tongues out at each other and got back to work.

Sara reached up and rang the bell that was hanging just above her. The ding reverberated across the whole place. "Sal! Phone call. He says he's an old friend."

Sal appeared just as the final tone died away, and rested his hands on the bar. "Which old friend?"

Sara looked good-heartedly at Sal and, with those deep brown eyes and a smile that could light up a room, said, "Like I know all your old friends. You make new friends every day and then tell me you've known them for years or something."

Sal laughed and grinned wide. "That's true, but with everyone being a friend, it's hard to have too many enemies." He moved from the bar to his office, saying over his shoulder, "Okay, transfer the call to my office."

Sal sat at his desk, smiled, and grabbed the receiver with a bounce of his fist and caught it in his other hand. "This is Sal. How long has it been since I've talked to my old friend?"

The raspy voice replied, "Saluto Salvatore."

Sal's face drained in color as he heard the voice at the other end of the call and clinched his free fist with knuckles popping. The jovial attitude he walked into the office with was gone. Now a steel tone replaced it. "Franco," and he paused with a more serious silence. "Not long enough."

"Now, don't be that way. I want to revisit what we spoke of the last time we met. You seem to have continued to do well for yourself." Franco's voice was dripping with what could only be taken as resentment.

"That was twenty years ago, Franco. I didn't need you as a partner then, and I don't need you as a partner now," Sal said with determination.

"No partnership this time. I want to buy the place. I'll offer you cash. All you have to do is sign it over."

With the same steely tone, Sal responded, "Quite the offer. But it's not for sale."

With what could only be taken as a smirk through the phone, Franco said, "Unfortunately, my capo unexpectedly died and left me the means with which to pursue my interests." Now it was Franco's turn to have a steel tone in his voice. "You remember our old capo, don't you? Why don't we get together and talk about it?"

This time Sal's face went red with rage. His voice was still as he spoke next. "I remember. I had great respect for him. He was honorable and did the right thing." Pausing and in a forced friendlier tone, Sal said, "We were friends... once, and I'll agree to hear you out. I have a poker game tonight at eleven. Come before the game, and we can talk."

The strong raspy voice said, "Prego, I'll be there."

With a heavy sigh and with what seemed to be a weight lifted off his shoulders, Sal ended the conversation with "Ciao." The line went silent.

Sal stood up, poured himself a long draw of bourbon that was on his desk, and swallowed it down in one pull. He picked up the receiver again and dialed a number. "John, this is Sal. I'm calling in a solid." As he did, he paused, looked up from the desk, and surveyed the office, taking it all in, and spoke. "I need your help with updating some documents for Sigaros and my will."

7

ood thing Sigaros was only a little ways away. I quickly locked up my bike off to the side of the building where nobody thinks to look, and rushed around to the front of the building and opened wide the double doors, and in a panting breath, bent over with my hands on my knees and winded I asked," Time!?"

Mia yelled out, "It's 1:59."

Kate dismissively called out, "I've got 2:01."

"I'll split it," I said, still panting. "Make it 2:00."

I finally found my breath, and with hands on my hips and with deep breaths in through my nose and out through my mouth, I made my way to the bar. Sara was still fixing up the bar. She was always working. Magically a cool glass of water appeared on the countertop in front of me as I approached. I looked gratefully at her and raised the glass to my lips. Never has anything tasted so cool as a drink of water in the Vegas heat. I set it down on the bar and, finally catching my breath, I looked at Sara and said, "Made it. Aren't you proud of me?"

"For being on time?" she said with her hands on her hips. "Oh yeah, real proud," this time dripping with sarcasm. She held up a thumb and pointed to the back. "Sal asked me to send you back when you came in."

"Already? Man, you put somebody in charge for one day, and they want to give you the riot act on what you did wrong." I pointed to the empty water glass, and Sara graciously filled it. She even curtsied. So I bowed. I turned back to the office after finishing the second glass; you have to stay hydrated. I spun on my heels back toward Sara and, in a whispered voice, asked, "You didn't tell him I forgot to lock up, did you?"

Not looking up from her work, she waved me away and whispered back, "No, now go. Sal seemed like he wanted to talk to you."

Still whispering, I answered back, "You're an angel, Sara," and blew her an audible kiss.

Sara turned this time, and with a furrowed brow, she pointed a finger to the office. Surprisingly just like my ma, and this time not in a whispered voice, said, "Get!"

I spun back around on my heels, straightened my shirt, buttoned the top button of my suit, and headed back. Sal was particular about the way people dressed. Not that he was big on fashion. However, anyone who worked for him always had to be presentable. That meant if you were in a suit when you were standing or walking around, it needed to be buttoned. In a two-button suit, the top one is always buttoned. In a three-button suit, the middle one is always buttoned, the top one is sometimes buttoned, and the bottom one is never buttoned. A lesson he told me the second day I met him. He had a whole story about ties as well. Given he never mandated I wear one, I only got that lecture once. Oh, and after what he told me about men never wearing a hat inside, I have refrained completely from all headwear.

Rapping my knuckles on the door lightly, I said, "It's Leo. You wanted to see me, boss?"

In the same calm voice he usually had, he answered, "Come in." He was standing, and it looked like he had just organized a stack of papers on his desk. "Good, you're on time. How did yesterday go?" This time he stopped and looked up at me.

I straightened up and reported the events of the day from when he left. After my fifteen-minute report on customers, bar receipts, distributors who dropped off supplies, and those who didn't, I ended it with, "Overall, it was a good day. Uneventful." I paused and thought back to how full the day felt and how smoothly it really did go. "I even had time to sit down and work on a few ideas for a business. I'd be happy to tell you about them."

He held up a hand in protest. "The distributor who didn't show. What's going on?"

"The Gurka Cigar distributor said he couldn't make it but would be here this afternoon. I talked him into throwing in two extra cases for our trouble."

Sal paused and sat at the end of his desk and, with a quizzical look, asked, "Two? I usually only get him to give me one. How'd you swing that?"

Straightening up again and pulling my suit down, I looked him straight in the eye, "Because I'm good. I told him that he has inconvenienced us, not just a business but me as a person and that his actions would lead to disturbing the customers at Sigaros who want their product. If they cannot supply our demands, we will go with a provider who can be reliable. I told him that I could have another distributor here by the end of the day."

With a look of approval, Sal crossed his arms and leaned back further onto his desk. "Is that so... and?"

With the same straight face, I answered, "And I said I'd put in a good word for him with Sara."

With the same stance and look, Sal said, "Does Sara know this?"

"No."

Sal smiled, shook his head, and stood up from the desk. "She's gonna hurt you, Leo, when she finds out. Make sure she knows what you did. She's not a piece of property to barter with. She's a friend, Leo. She'll be mad. But it's the action of doing the right thing that's important regardless of the consequences."

I loosened my shoulders a little and shifted my weight where I stood. I couldn't argue with Sal on that. Sara wasn't property to be bargained with. I'll have to fix this. "Fine. I'll tell her the guy's sweet on her and that he may try to flirt with her next time he's in."

"And you gave him the impression it was okay. Right, Leo?"

"And I may have given him that impression." *Man, she was gonna hurt me. I'll cross that bridge when it happens.*

"You did a satisfactory job running the place," with a nod of his head. "Well done. You even locked up. Don't let the distributors waste your time today. I'll be out the rest of the day. Place is yours to run. I'll be back before the end of closing for tonight's poker game."

I was a little surprised to see Sal heading out again for the day. He'd never been gone that much, let alone two days in a row. "Sure, Sal. Anything you need me to do while you're gone?"

Grabbing the stack of papers from his desk, he looked up. "Just take care of the place. I'm trusting you."

This time I nodded. "Got it, boss. Oh, who's coming to the game tonight? Gino and the rest of the guys?"

Sal stopped midway across the office on his way to the door and turned, looking at the fireplace mantle. "Some old friends will be here tonight. You haven't met them."

Like I said, I like to push my limits and see how far I can take the old man. "I'd like to come to the game sometime."

This time turning to look at me, he paused, and with a sincere tone said, "One day. Not tonight. Stakes are a little too high on this game."

With a shrug, I answered. "I respect that. Hopefully, in a few months, one of my ideas will pan out, and I'll have enough cash to play in the game."

This time in a somber tone, as though he was thinking about something else entirely, "I hope so too."

With the papers in hand, he moved toward the fireplace. Now I knew he had a safe behind his desk, but when Sal placed his thumb on the side, a small drawer popped open that was built into the brick mantle, and I felt like I was invading his privacy somehow. "Want me to leave, boss?"

Looking over his shoulder, in that same somber tone, he said, "No, you stay for this." He let me watch him open the small compartment. It couldn't have held much as it was only the size of two of the bricks. He pulled out what looked like a leather notebook that was held closed with a leather strap and put it into his inside coat pocket. He turned and looked around the room in what seemed to be a long pause.

Sal doesn't often get sentimental or somber, and this was starting to seem odd. "You okay, boss?"

Shaking out of the movement this time, Sal straightened up and looked bigger than usual, somehow. "I'm fine. Just taking it all in." He came over and slapped me on the shoulder. Grabbing his hat and coat off the rack, he strolled to the door and was gone.

I took a minute to process Sal's reactions. That was different. I guess as you get older, you get all sentimental. Strange. I walked out of the office and headed to the bar. I was tapping my fingers on the bar, looking at the closed entryway doors from where Sal had just left, and was again processing those last moments in the office. Why did he let me see him open up that drawer in the fireplace?

Sara must have seen my look and nudged my shoulder as she exited the bar, heading to one of the tables to help the twins. "Where's he going again?"

Still looking at the doors, I replied, "Said he needed to go out again, and that he'd be back before closing." This time breaking my look away from the door, I tilted my head as Sara walked back around behind me and grinned, saying, "He said that the place is mine to run."

She looked at me again, rolled her eyes, and got back to work. The day went on as usual; nothing eventful; customers came and went; drinks were drunk, and a good time was had by all it seemed. Until the Gurkha cigar distributor arrived. *Oh crap!* I thought to myself. *Sara's gonna kill me.* The guy looked so happy when he got up to the bar after putting all the boxes away. Its gonna crush him to tell him I didn't talk to Sara. I looked up at the ceiling and in my head said, "Why does doing the responsible thing suck so much! That's why I'm going to find someone to run things when I have a business and just sit back."

I took a deep breath in and exhaled, and made my way to where Tony, the distributor, was standing at the opposite end of the bar. I placed my hand on Tony's shoulder. He couldn't have been more than five six and was a well-built fit Spanish American. He turned and looked and smiled up at me, saying, "Extra boxes are on the center countertop in the humidor. There's actually three. Thanks for putting in a good word for me with Sara."

Oh man, he really did have a thing for Sara. This was gonna be rough. I smiled back at him and said, "Yeah. About that." I waved Sara over from the other end of the bar as she was finishing with a customer, and she made her way over. She really did look great in those black skintight jeans and boots. It was like watching a runway model approach you. I could hear Tony audibly gulp. Had I not felt like a shmuck, I might have done the same thing.

"What's up, Leo? Can I help?" she said with a smile looking between Tony and I.

Straightening up and making sure both could see me, I said, "Sara, this is Tony. He's one of the distributors. I lied to him yesterday." This time they both looked at me, surprised. "I told Tony I would put in a good word about him with you. He was late on a shipment, and I bargained for an extra supply and pushed it further by saying I would put in a good word for him with you. Tony, I should never have done that. You are a nice guy, but it is not my place to introduce you to a woman or put you in their good graces. You can do that on your own. I am sorry, and please take any extra boxes back that you delivered. If you like, I will be happy to compensate you or the company for any inconvenience."

Tony stared at me, puzzled, and a flush of embarrassment showed in his cheeks, and he looked down at the bar.

I turned to Sara and saw a redness growing in her face. "Sara, I apologize for my actions. You are a person and not a piece of property for me to exchange goods. I was wrong. My intentions were not respectful. I see my error and want to correct it. If Tony was interested, I should have asked if you felt similarly and arranged an introduction only then." The redness in her face was still there. However, it stopped rising just short of her forehead.

I turned to both of them. "I apologize for any embarrassment that I caused either one of you. Please, any anger felt should be directed toward me, not at each other."

There was a long pause, and Tony was still looking flushed, and his eyes were trying to avoid Sara's and mine. Sara looked straight at me, and I didn't leave her gaze. I was waiting for a slap or punch in the nose or for her to scream at me, but she just kept staring at me. She looked at Tony, saw his embarrassment, and in a kind tone said, "Tony, next time you want to get to know a woman, come up and introduce yourself. That action alone speaks for you and is better than any good word from someone else."

In a meek voice, Tony said, "You're right. I apologize to you. I was just nervous and wanted to talk to you."

Sara took a deep breath and rolled her eyes at me. She slapped the bar playfully to get Tony to look up and shake him out of his embarrassment. "Tony, I'm going to buy you a drink. What'll you have?"

Tony looked at me, then Sara. "A rum and coke, please. May I ask if you'd like to join me for a drink as well?"

Sara smiled, and I saw the flush fade away from Tony's cheeks. "I can't drink on the job, but I would love to talk with you while you had yours."

"That'd be great," Tony said with a wide smile.

I left the two of them to talk without saying a word. *That was tough.* The action of doing the right thing... what's Sal thinking? "I think she's still gonna hurt me," I said to myself, walking away. Before we had finished, the old receiver rang next to the bar. Mike, seeing we were in a serious conversation, chose not to yell out for Sara or I.

Mike put down the tray of empty glassware, wiped his hand on the bar towel, and picked up the receiver. "Sigaros. This is Mike. How can I help?"

"It's Sal. I need to talk to Leo or Sara."

"They're just with a customer. I'll go get Leo."

"No, don't interrupt them. Let Leo know I'll be back after closing and that the place is to be locked up at ten. Sharp! I've got an important poker game."

"Sure, boss. Okay, I'll give him the message. Got it." Mike hung up the phone just as I was walking up.

In a rushed voice, Mike relayed the message. "It was Sal. He said he'll be back after closing and to close at ten sharp. He was very specific about closing right at ten. Said it was an important poker game."

I looked at Mike, still thinking about the conversation I had with Tony and Sara, and saw that it was already nine. In a flat tone, I said, "Don't worry I'll sound the bell just before ten to let everybody know it's closing time."

When the bell sounded, everybody in the place looked up as I called out, "Last call." The regulars took their drinks. The last cigar customer came and went by nine forty-five. I worked in the bar taking care of customers, organized all the receipts, and helped the twins and Mike until Tony and Sara finished talking at about nine fifty. Looked like they were having a nice time. I was glad they were okay with each other.

Tony waved bye to Sara from the door and yelled back to me with a big smile. "No hard feelings, Leo! See you next month with the delivery." I smiled and waved back, glad to see he didn't seem to bear me any ill will.

Sara walked up to me with that same runway model approach. I put down the glass I was cleaning and faced her. She stood one foot away from me, pointed a finger right in my face, and with a firm voice said, "You ever do something like that again, and you'll walk with a limp the rest of your life. Got it? You're lucky you apologized before anything happened."

This time I gulped audibly. She turned and picked up the glass next to mine and pointed to the towel I set down when she approached for me to get back to cleaning. I picked up the glass and towel and said, "I'm sorry, Sara. I won't do that again."

She didn't look up from cleaning the glass and said in a quiet tone, "Apology accepted. Tony was okay. Shy and quirky and not my type but okay. He has a lot in common with a girlfriend of mine, and I'm going to ask her if she'd like to meet up together next week."

With a smile and a hopeful expression, I said, "That's great. I'm glad."

I turned to put the glass down. Sara did too. "Oh, one other thing, Leo." She punched me in my right arm hard enough for a shock to go down to my fingers, and I visibly grimaced.

I had that coming. I believed her when she said she'd make me walk with a limp if I really upset her. "Really? With the right?"

She smiled wryly and looked at me, batting those brown eyes. "You're lucky that was my right. I'm a lefty."

Rubbing my arm, I smiled back and went back to closing up. Thank goodness it was Monday, and we were closing by ten. *I think as soon as I get home, I'm going to sleep until tomorrow afternoon.* I walked everyone out and said my goodbyes and then, without having to be told by Sara this time, turned and locked up, dropped the keys in my pocket, and headed for my bicycle.

Sara stopped me and yelled for me to put it in the back of her Jeep, saying she'd give me a ride home. I looked up and thanked the stars for yet one more reprieve at the end of this day. The drive home was calm but not cool. The Vegas heat will still out radiating up from the asphalt, but it was cooler than the daytime. The sun wasn't baking you from above anymore.

Sara shifted the gear shift in the Wrangler. "How did it feel?" she asked.

I tilted my head and looked at her, rubbing my arm. "It hurt! Thank you very much."

Rolling her eyes, she said, "No. Taking responsibility for Sigaros, for your actions?"

I looked ahead and said, "Well..." I had to pause because somewhere deep down, it felt all right. I thought taking charge while Sal was gone was going to be annoying, to be honest, but the day flew by again, and everything seemed to fall into its place. "Felt all right," I said in a surprised tone and looked at her.

She nodded, gripping the wheel. "I'm glad. It suited to you. Running the place today... and apologizing to Tony and I."

I smiled at her with a big goofy grin, and without looking at me, she told me to shut up. We pulled up to the house, and she looked the place over. "Nice spot."

I looked down and opened the Jeep door, and got my bicycle. "It's just temporary. Hoping to get my own place soon enough."

Sara started the Jeep back up. "It's nice to have family. Not everybody has that. Be thankful you do."

I looked at her a little longer than I should have, and she looked back at me, then popped the clutch and drove away. I walked inside after parking my bike and put my coat and button-down shirt on the chair. I grabbed a glass of water and headed up to my room. I immediately found that nice cool pillow I'd been thinking about all morning and fell soundly asleep.

8

I swear it felt like I just laid my head down on the pillow. A buzzing noise kept interrupting what was proving to be the nicest sleep I'd had in the past few days. I lazily opened one eye, lifted my head off the pillow, and searched for my phone by following that buzzing annoyance. I finally grabbed it and held it to my chest with a deep sigh, waiting for my eyes to focus in the dim light of my room, and looked down at the phone. Eleven o'clock. Wow, I must have been exhausted. I blinked a few times and looked at my phone more closely. Four missed phone calls and ten texts. Panicking in my mind. *Did I forget something? Oh man, I know I locked up.* I sat up in bed, adjusted my clothes, went to the window, and opened the curtains to let the brightness of the day fill the room. Then I opened my phone. Surprisingly, I had missed calls from Sara and from Mickey's restaurant as well as texts from Sara and the twins. The last call was from Sara not two minutes ago. I pressed redial.

Sara picked up before the end of one ring. In a rushed voice, she almost leapt out of the phone at me. "Where are you, Leo? I've been trying to get you for the last hour." But now, with more concern in her voice and a catch in her throat, she said, "I thought... I thought something happened to you too."

I blinked a few more times. She was serious and concerned.

"What's going on? What are you talking about? I just woke up and saw all these messages from you, the twins, and I think Gino tried calling me," I said, perplexed.

"It's Sal. He's..." All I could hear was sobbing on the other end of the line.

My heart sank. As calmly as I could, I said, "Sara, take a breath. What happened? Where are you?"

I heard her try and pause and catch her breath, still crying. "Sal's dead," she said in a whimper. I felt sick to my stomach and found myself having to sit down immediately. "I'm here in front of Sigaros with Gino, Mike, Mia, and Kate, and the rest of the people from the plaza."

I bowed my head and took a breath. Crying a little harder this time, she said, "Leo. Someone shot him. The police are all over Sigaros."

My head started to swirl. I could feel goose bumps all over my body, and my pulse started to quicken. A race of thoughts collected in my mind. *How could he be dead? Someone shot him? It was Sal. No one could take on Sal. Who'd want to? Everyone loved him.* I could feel my body start to tense up all over, and my anger start to boil up.

In what I thought was a calm voice through gritted teeth, I told her, "I'll be right there." I could still hear her sniffling. I didn't like hearing her this way. I took a deep breath and unclenched my jaw. "I'm on my way, Sara. Tell everyone I'm on my way."

I heard a final sniffle and a brief "Okay."

The room was so quiet and still. It was such a stark contrast to the flurry of thoughts in my head. I needed to get to Sigaros. I took the fastest shower I've ever taken and threw on a button-down shirt and slacks. I raced down the stairs and grabbed my suit coat.

My parents were in the kitchen, and they both looked down at their watches.

Ma said, "You're going to work now? It's not two."

Without pausing to look, I opened the door and yelled back, "I need to get in early. It's important." I unplugged the bicycle, straddled the seat, and put the pedals in motion as the electric motor kicked in, and I took off for Sigaros.

9

I made it there in record time. The whole way over, all I could think of was that this was a dream. He couldn't be dead. And shot? Why? Did it have something to do with yesterday and why he was going out? Did it have to do with that drawer in the fireplace? I rounded the last street and found myself in the cul-de-sac. There were police cars, an ambulance, a coroner's car, a Channel 5 News van, and all the regular customers' own vehicles. I tossed my bike off to the side near a police car and rushed up to the small crowd that had formed just in front of Sigaros, which was blocked off by police tape.

It wasn't hard to find Sara. She was holding onto the twins, and Gino was placing his arms around their shoulders.

As I was running up, I saw Mike the barback running toward me from the opposite direction with hands outstretched. "What happened? Sara told me to get down here now," he said, barely out of breath and following behind me as I headed toward Sara and the twins.

"No clue, Mike. All I heard was Sal was dead," I said as I picked up my step. I heard him stop. I stopped short too. He didn't know. Crap. He shouldn't have had to find out like that. I walked back to him and put a hand on his shoulder. "Come on. Let's go. Let's figure out what happened." In a daze, Mike shook his head, kept quiet, and followed me.

Mia was the first to see me. She ran over. I bent down, and she hugged me around the neck. She was shaking. Kate came over and put a hand on Mia's back, and let go after a moment. I looked down at Mia, and she looked a mess. Tears and mascara were streaming down her face. I held her shoulder, and we all walked over to the front of the police tape where Gino and Sara were watching the front door to Sigaros.

I tapped Gino and Sara on the shoulders. He stuck out his hand; we shook and met glances. I could tell Sal's old friend was upset. Not crying but visibly shaken. Sara, on the other hand, punched me with her left hand in my upper chest.

"Hey!" I said loud enough to be heard by others around me and then lowered my voice. "What was that for?" I said in a more hushed and surprised voice.

In a whisper, she said, "Where the hell have you been? I was worried you were with Sal. The police won't tell us anything."

"I was at home. Asleep." Looking around the group, I stared at each one of them. "Why would I be with Sal?"

Leaning into our little group so that the other bystanders wouldn't hear, Sara said quietly, "Because Sal messaged me last night just after I dropped you off asking if the place was closed up, and he said he was going to contact you because he needed your help with something."

I fumbled for my phone in my suit coat and opened my messages. I had texts from Mia, Kate, and Sara but nothing from Sal. I turned to show the group my message list. "Nothing and no voicemails. What time exactly did he message you?"

This time Sara pulled her phone out from her back pocket and scanned her messages quickly. "It was at 10:45."

I looked up at the door to Sigaros and, with hands on my hips, said aloud to the group, not looking at anyone, "Strange. That's right in the middle of the poker game. He usually doesn't use his phone when he's playing poker."

This time Gino spoke up and looked at me oddly, tilting his head questioning my last statement. "Sal canceled the game last night. He asked me to call the other guys to let them know it was off. Said something came up."

Mike nervously spoke this time. "No, no. He told me he had an important poker game. He said for me to tell Leo to close at ten sharp." Turning to me in protest, he said, "Honest, he told me he had a game."

I put my hand back on his shoulder and looked him in the eye. "I believe you. He told me the same thing before he left yesterday." Mike seemed to calm down.

Why would he cancel the game? I wondered.

Gino leaned into the group and started to speak in a hushed voice. "I got here at nine thirty this morning and saw the door to Sigaros was open a crack. It's never open that early. I opened it up." This time Gino's voice cracked. "Sal was on the ground just as I walked in. There was so much blood. He had four bullet holes in his back. The place was a mess, with chairs and tables turned over from the front door heading to his office. I rushed over to him and... and he was gone." Looking down, he finished with that same crack in his voice. "I called the police, then Sara and you, Leo... Sal was gone." We were all silent.

Just then, a man approached the police tape. He was an African American of average height and average build and was a little more than middle-aged with salt-and-pepper hair. "I'm Detective Thomas. Are you all the staff of Sigaros?"

I spoke up. "We are, except Gino. He's the owner of the restaurant just next door." I pointed over to the steakhouse.

Gino spoke up, clearing his voice. "I own Mickey's. My name is Luigino Rossi. I was a friend of Sal's. I was the one found him and called the police."

Detective Thomas nodded. "Thank you, Mr. Rossi. I'd like to start by asking you some questions. I'd like to ask all of you some questions one-on-one. Please stay here, and we'll call each of you to give a statement." He then proceeded to take down each of our names, numbers, and addresses.

The detective turned to walk away, waving for Gino to follow him. "Detective Thomas," Gino said as he crossed under the police tape. "Can they wait in my restaurant? We all just lost a friend. They could do to get inside and sit down."

The detective turned and looked at each of us and nodded and said to two uniformed officers standing in front of Mickey's, "Let these people in and wait at the front door. Inside with them." He said it as if to a child so that all his instructions were followed. He turned back to us and waved us through. I raised the tape, and all of us headed for Mickey's, each one of us looking at the door of Sigaros.

10

We all somberly walked into Mickey's steakhouse.

Mia was still pretty upset and shaking. "Mike, give me a hand with these chairs. We'll put them around this table."

Mike was a good guy. He was holding up. He hopped to it and had the chairs set out, and pulled two out for Mia and Kate. I walked around to the bar, pulled down a bottle of brandy, poured a small amount into a snifter, and set it down in front of Mia. She took it gratefully and, in between drying her eyes, sipped at the drink. I sat down next to Sara while Mike and Kate tried to talk to Mia and comfort each other.

I turned to Sara, and her face was starting to turn red. I was a little worried I was going to get hit again. She leaned into me a little and, in a quiet but firm voice, said, "Next time I call you, answer your phone right away!" She turned, looking out into space. "I can't believe he's gone." Then turned to me again. "I thought something happened to you. I didn't know what to do or who to call. I told the twins and then sent a message to Mike." This time looking down in pain. "I felt so bad having to tell Mia and Kate. Oh no! I forgot to call the distributors to tell them they can't come by today. I have to..."

I grabbed her hands, saying, "Stop! You don't have to do anything right now. Just be here in this moment." I could see the tears starting to build.

"But I can't. I need to do something, or all I'll think about is that Sal's gone."

In my most calming voice, I told her, "We will all get through this together."

Just then, Gino walked through the door. He pointed to Sara and said the detective wanted to see her. She grabbed my hands tightly and stood up. She walked away with the poise she always had. I even think I saw the two officers who held the doors open for her gulp when she walked by.

Gino sat down next to me and let out a deep sigh.

In a whisper, I asked, "How'd it go, Gino?"

"Fine. He doesn't know what happened. It's too early. He asked all the regular stuff," he said, a little exasperated.

"Regular stuff? You've been asked about a murder by a detective before?"

Gino looked at me as if I was the crazy one. "Well... yeah. It is Vegas."

I was shocked. "What the hell does that mean, Gino?"

"It means that I wasn't always a restaurant owner and that I have a past. Not a murderous past, but a past that had some run-ins with, let's say, less desirables. That's how I met Sal."

Still shocked, I raised my voice. "What?" The two officers looked over. Gino and I smiled at them, and they went back to looking after the door.

Through gritted teeth, Gino said, "Keep it down."

In a rushed, whispered voice, I asked, "What do you mean that's how you met Sal?"

Looking around him, Gino leaned in. "Listen, it's not my place to talk about Sal's past, nor is this the time to go into it. Let's just say Sal and I found ourselves in jobs we didn't expect and no longer wanted to continue with, and we wound up leaving that life more than thirty years ago."

The police officers started to look over, and Gino raised a hand to his lips. When the officers turned away, he said, "Somebody has to go tell Valentino about Sal."

Amazed by the last few statements, I held up my hands. "Who is Valentino?"

Whispering back at me, he said, "Sal's brother!"

"Sal had a brother?"

"Yeah. He's a priest across town. Where do you think he went every Sunday?"

"He never said anything about that or his possible seedy past, Gino," I said in an accusatory tone.

Gino raised his hands up in concession. "Sal kept a few things close to his chest. I'm not denying that. Not many people still around that know us older guys... or our families."

"Why don't you go tell Valentino if you know him?"

With hesitation in his voice, Gino said, "Valentino and I... don't see eye to eye."

"Why not?" I asked, sitting up in my chair.

"I have my reasons." Gino saw the look on my face. "Nothing... that bad. Sal's not the only one who kept a few things close to his chest." With that, Gino stood up and said, "I have to make a few phone calls on Sal's behalf. There are people in and out of town who will want to know." In a kind tone, Gino said, "Please go tell Valentino about Sal."

Before I could protest, Sara walked back in and hurried over to the table as they called for Mia and Kate to go speak to the detective.

Sara sat down next to me and leaned in close, turning her head away from the front door so that the officers couldn't hear her speak. "The place was an absolute mess." Catching herself choke up, she said, "Sal was gone, but I could see all the tables and chairs overturned. The detective has no clue who killed Sal. He kept asking me if Sal had any enemies, or if there is anybody who wanted to hurt him, or if there were any odd phone calls or changes in his behavior."

"What did you tell him?"

Sara looked at me with her hands up. "I told him what happened. Nothing. Everything was business as usual. I told him the bar was running well. Everybody was happy. Nobody was causing a problem. Regular phone calls. Just like the one we got the other day."

"What call the other day?"

"Right before you came in. Before you were almost late," she said, grinning at me for the first time that day. "An old friend of Sal's called with a real raspy voice asking to talk with him."

"Which old friend?"

Exasperated, Sara, with a hand on her hip, said, "Like I know each one of his old friends. Sal and you are the same. You were…"

I touched her hand after she trailed away. "Was that right before he asked to see me?"

With wide eyes, she said, "Yes. Yes, it was. Do you think that has something to do with this?"

I leaned back in my chair. "Maybe. Did you tell the detective that Sal went out for the day?"

"Yes, I did. I told him he left you in charge and that he did that the day before."

"Does he know that Sal didn't typically do that?"

Shaking her head, she said, "I didn't think it meant anything. He didn't ask me, and I didn't tell him."

Leaning further back in my chair, I thought about the other day with the papers in that drawer by the fireplace. "Did Detective Thomas say if anything was missing? Did he say if the safe was open?"

"I didn't think to ask. What are you thinking about, Leo?"

I tapped her knee and leaned in to tell her more when the officers asked for me to go over as Mia and Kate were coming back in. "I'll tell you when I get back. Did you know Sal had a brother?"

Surprised, she said, "He has a brother? I've been here a little over four years... I never knew that. Are you sure?"

Pointing across the restaurant over at Gino, I said, "Yeah, he just told me."

I got up and then walked toward the door, nodding at the two officers as they held the door open. I turned to my left and walked up to the front door of Sigaros. I didn't know if I was ready to see the place just yet. I knocked, and Detective Thomas called me in. Just as you enter Sigaros, there's a small foyer with a double door that provides a break from the heat of Las Vegas before you enter the more tropical coolness of the main room. That's where Detective Thomas and I met. You could clearly see through those glass double doors how turned over everything looked inside. I couldn't see where Sal's body was before they took him out, and I didn't want to look.

Detective Thomas saw me looking over the place and cleared his throat. I looked back in his direction and straightened my suit. "Leonard, correct?"

"Yes, detective," I said calmly.

"Run me through yesterday."

I ran through the day's events, from the regular customers to the distributors to any phone calls I could remember, except the one that Sarah spoke of the day prior. I finished with the message from Sal asking to close up at ten o'clock.

"Was that odd for him to say?"

"No, it was pretty common. He had a poker game Monday nights, and he typically liked the place empty before it started."

"But he canceled that game."

"I didn't know that."

Looking down at his pad and scribbling a note, Detective Thomas said in a questioning tone, "Mr. Salvatore Accardi didn't tell his manager that he had canceled his poker game?"

I looked at the detective, confused at his last statement. "Manager? What are you talking about?"

"You're the manager. It says so on the paperwork from his desk. It goes back for the last two weeks, citing a change in your status from security to manager of Sigaros."

I was surprised. "I... well... he had asked me to take care of the place when he was not around just two days ago."

"Regardless, he has you listed here as manager." The detective reached out and handed me a paper. There it was in Sal's handwriting. "Leonard: Job title: Manager."

I looked down at the paper. It was from Sal's books that he kept in the safe. "Huh. How'd you like that?" I said, still surprised. "So, the safe was open." I looked up at the detective. This time he stopped writing in his pad and looked up at me. "Was anything taken?"

"Why would you say the safe was open?" the detective asked matter-of-factly.

"Sal put his books away every night. He didn't leave them out on his desk. This paper is from one of his ledgers. The six months I've been here, he never once left this out."

The detective nodded. "The locks on the front door weren't damaged. The office safe was open, and it didn't look like it was forced. Seems as though a struggle started there and made its way to the front. Looks like he fought whomever it was back all the way to the front of the place. There was more than one other person here besides him. Maybe three, based on some of the forensic findings... He was shot once in the chest and then four times in the back."

I looked back over through the glass doors. *Sounds about right,* I thought. *It would've taken more than three guys to keep Sal down.* Then that ache in my stomach when I first heard he'd been shot set in again, thinking about what Sara told me. He needed my help. Maybe if I had been here, he wouldn't be dead. Who the heck shot him? And why?

Drawing my attention back with another clearing of his throat, Detective Thomas asked, "Did Mr. Accardi keep anything else in the safe besides the ledgers? A gun, money, any object?"

"Sal didn't like guns. I never saw one in there. I left the day's money in a security bag below the register on a shelf. Sal usually picked it up when he came in and put it in the safe."

The detective waved to one of the forensic personnel and pointed them over to the cash register to look. The bag was there.

"Odd that he didn't put it away, isn't it?" said the detective.

"Yeah, it's usually the first thing he did before heading to the office," I said looking back over, asking the same question in my head.

In a somewhat accusatory tone, he said, "So, you've seen the safe and its contents before. Seems like, for someone who was just made aware he was manager, you knew a lot about the day-to-day operations and the personal patterns of the owner and its staff."

I looked down at him. I turned my head and replied, "Yeah, Sal asked me to help with security. Anyone who's supposed to work security would figure those things out, or else they're bad at their job."

"I see," he said, looking back down at his notepad, not looking up at me.

I was annoyed, and then it dawned on me. "What's the deal? Are you trying to say I had something to do with this?!" and I took a step forward, feeling my anger starting to build.

Noticing me taking a step forward, Detective Thomas raised his voice and dropped his right hand back, and held his left hand out with his pad to stop me. "Hey! Take a step back. Now!"

Two police officers popped the doors open immediately with eyes on me and hands on their sidearms.

I stopped and raised my hands. "Sorry." And I took a step back. "I'm just... just upset. Sal was a friend. He was a good person." I thought for a moment more and paused as the flash of what he really was entered my head. "He... was a mentor."

Waving the officers away and retracting his right arm, Detective Thomas said, "Understandable. But I'm trying to get to the bottom of this murder. I need to know the circumstances of Mr. Accardi's current events." Looking back down at his notepad, he followed up with, "I already know his history."

Surprised at the last statement, I asked, "I'm sorry? His history? He's owned Sigaros since the seventies. That's his past."

Dryly, the detective looked up. "Your mentor…" this time he scoffed as he flipped back through his notes "… as you call him, was not always the owner of this place. He was muscle for one of the mob families back in Cleveland. He's had a few misdemeanors and was implied in one felony that was dismissed."

The scoff pissed me off, but I was too stunned about hearing he was muscle for the mob. *What the hell, Sal? That couldn't have been you.*

The detective went on. "That's probably how he got this place," waving his pad around dismissively. "It appears his past may have come back to haunt him for any of his selfish and ill deeds.

I stood up to my full height and, without realizing it, I had closed my fists tightly. The only reason I knew was the popping sound my knuckles made. A voice started to build in the back of my mind that, for some reason, sounded like Sal. It started to say over and over again, "Don't hit the cop. It's just his job. Don't hit the cop." Great! Now my conscience was starting to sound like Sal. Gritting my teeth, I asked, "Are we done?"

The detective looked down at my knuckles and then, I think for the first time, realized how tall I was. He wouldn't have had time to call out this time. I was closer than the last time he stopped me. He just looked up. Calmly he said, "We're done. For now."

He motioned his arm to the door, and I turned and pushed both doors open, and in doing so, physically moved both officers off their balance, making when they looked back up at me all that more satisfying. I could see they knew I was pissed. I stuck my hand out before one of the doors shut and looked over my shoulder, asking, "How long will Sigaros be closed?"

Detective Thomas looked up and, in that same calm voice, said, "Until the murder is solved."

I nodded and let the door close. The officers made way for me to walk out, and I headed back to Mickey's restaurant.

11

With my blood still boiling, I opened the restaurant doors and walked through the middle of the entryway. Everyone stopped their conversations and just looked. They didn't say a word. They all watched me closely, especially the two officers. As I turned my gaze to the left, I found what I was looking for.

Gino was behind the bar. Looking at me while still talking on the phone, he reached under from where he was standing and pulled out a bottle of Redbreast. Whiskey was his drink of choice. I kept walking toward him. I guess my fists were still clenched because as I raised them to grab one of the two drinks he poured, I had to consciously open my hands, relieving some of the tension in my arms. I raised the glass. Gino's glass rang against mine with the tone only noticed in well-crafted drinkware. I took my drink down. I opened my mouth, let the fire of the drink escape, and with it, some of the anger I'd been wanting to release. My anger was lingering, and when I said "Thank you," it must have come out a little steely because Gino paused on the phone and pointed at my empty glass. Like at a blackjack table, I waved my hand for a pass.

I met his gaze. I wanted answers. What was that detective going on about regarding Sal's past? "When you're done, I want to talk."

Gino nodded, not looking away, and I turned away, facing the others in the room.

I wanted to talk to my friends. I needed to process what just happened, what I was just told. I was surprised to see them all staring. Mike, Mia, and Kate all shrugged their shoulders and looked away when I met their gaze. Only Sara looked back at me and didn't look away—just tilted her head questioning my entrance.

"What?" I asked to the question in their expressions.

In a nervous tone, Mike spoke up. "What happened? You looked like you were going to tear someone apart." Looking down again, he spoke. "Maybe you should sit and... and take a breather."

Rubbing her arms like she was cold, Mia spoke up now, finally looking at me but not quite meeting my eyes, and said, "Yeah, Leo, Sal wouldn't want you to get into trouble just 'cause you were angry."

That did it. Mia saying that in that sweet voice dripping with concern. She was right; Sal wouldn't have wanted that. My shoulders started to loosen.

I bent my head down. "True." I lumbered over to sit down next to Sara and Mia as the police officer motioned for Mike to go see Detective Thomas. I felt a weariness set in from the draw of alcohol and the rush of adrenaline leaving my body.

Mike sprung up, looking at everyone and then at me. His fingers were starting to twitch.

They all started to look at me again. This time with the look of people needing answers. "Mike. It'll be all right. There isn't a wrong answer."

In a rushed voice, Mike let out, "But what about the phone call? About the poker game. Sal said he was going to have one."

I held up a hand to stop him. Sara jumped in. "Just tell them the truth. That's all. You can't get into trouble for telling the truth."

Mike nodded and looked at the girls, and Kate gave him a quick smile and went back to talking to Mia.

Sara turned, leaning in close to me so that no one else would hear. I could smell her jasmine perfume. Smells can conjure up so many memories and emotions. In this moment, it felt like everything slowed down, and it was intoxicating. My adrenaline must have still been running high because when she leaned in, I noticed my pulse quicken again.

Looking at me with those deep brown eyes, she asked, "What happened?"

I paused and took in the moment. She felt so close. My body started to loosen up. Feeling less argumentative than my recent conversation with Detective Thomas, I looked down. A feeling of regret set in as I was finally able to take a step back. I knew what had just happened.

"Nothing." Shaking my head, I said, "The detective got the better of me. He was saying something about Sal's past, and it got me... pissed off." I rubbed my hands on my face and placed them on my knees in reflection. "I guess he had to ask his questions."

She slapped my hand. Not hard, like I knew she could have. I've taken two good punches from her recently, and I knew this wasn't angry. She was annoyed.

I looked up.

"Don't let that happen. You shouldn't let someone goad you into reacting like a goon."

I sat up a little in the chair and thought to myself, a goon? Maybe a hothead or easily excitable, but I'm not a goon. I looked at her with widened eyes. "Goon?"

"Well, you sure had the look of one with that stoic walk and that deep "Thank you." Like you were going to breathe fire on them with that drink."

I grinned. "I'll... pay attention next time."

This time she grabbed my hand for a moment. It was warm and comforting. The moment lingered for only a moment and passed as soon as she let go. It would've been nice to stay that way a little longer.

I straightened up and turned to include all of them in my next question. "Do any of you know what Sal did before owning Sigaros?"

Sara was the first to speak. "I always thought he bought the place from a prior owner. There are some photos in his office when he first started, and it looks that way. Why?"

I scratched my head. What was the detective talking about? I looked over at Gino. He was still on the telephone.

Looking back at them all, I said, "Nothing, just something Detective Thomas said that was... different." Pausing, I turned to the twins. "Mia, Kate, how about you?"

Kate spoke up first. "From what Mia and I could figure out, we think Sal was from out of town and then bought the place somehow back in the seventies. Some of the older customers would talk about how the place turned around when Sal took over back then and how much better things turned out here and around the area." Mia nodded her head in agreement, still rubbing her arms.

I sat back and took in what they each had to say. It told me none of them knew what he did before Sigaros. I wanted to talk to Gino, but he was still on the phone. I sat and nodded. I guess they should know what Detective Thomas said about our place.

With a sigh, I let out, "Sigaros will be closed until the murder is solved. That's what the detective said. He's working on figuring out a few different things about Sal's... murder." That last word hung heavily in the air, and when I said it, it sat in my stomach harder than I thought.

With glassy and distant eyes, Mia spoke up. "I think it was a robbery. They wanted the money and Sal... poor Sal..." sniffling again as she spoke. "He tried to defend the place." Now sobbing again, Kate pulled her into her arms. "He should've just let them have the money. It wasn't worth it."

Kate just held her and said, "We know. It could've been a robbery, Mia."

Sara sat back. "I don't know. I can't figure it out what happened last night. We don't have enough of the story. We need more information." Looking at me, she paused. "I-I think we should ask around." Now looking at the group, she said, "I think somebody wanted to take Sigaros from Sal, and the only way to do it was to kill him."

The room was quiet again. We were all thinking it. If someone did want to take Sigaros from Sal, that would've been the only way. It was his. It was a part of him. It was his home.

Mia looked up, tears finally drying. "What are we gonna do? I don't want to work anywhere else. I can't see Sigaros shutting down. It's like home."

Still holding her sister, Kate said in a comforting tone, "It'd be a shame, but realistically, we can't open it. Sal was the owner."

Sara chimed in. "But in a place of business, a manager can keep a place open for business reasons until legal proceedings take place or until a partner or another owner is identified. We've gone over this in one of my law classes."

I guess I could keep the place open, but I'm not sure I want to. I feel bad for Sara and Mike and the twins, but maybe I could just cut my losses and move on. Why stay? If I stay to keep the place open, I'd have to figure out a murder. What if I get hurt? No way. It's too much.

I looked up, and Mia, Kate, and Sara looked so defeated. Just then, Gino came over. He sat and let out a large puff of air. Gino felt the sense of defeat hanging in the air. "I'm so sorry, everyone. Sal was a good person. A great friend. It won't be the same without him. Knew him for the better part of four decades."

I met his eyes. He was heartbroken as well. Just then, Mike entered the restaurant and was heading back over to the table. I took the opportunity to mouth silently to Gino, "We need to talk about Sal." Gino shook his head and placed a finger on his lips, looking over at the officer's direction. I took the hint. Not here. Not now.

Got it. Does that mean there's something the cops shouldn't hear? If so, what?

Mike reached the table and started up nervously again, "Detective Thomas said we could all go." He closed his eyes, remembering word for word what the detective told him to tell us. "But we're not to leave town and that he might call us in again for further questioning and that he has our contact information." We all looked around and started to stand, and Mike shouted out, "Oh! And that the manager of Sigaros should give him the keys to the place. He asked for you, Leo."

They all looked around. I hadn't gotten to the part about me being manager. I jingled the keys out of my pocket and looked down at the main key and the spare, and placed them on the table.

Sara looked at me, questioning Mike's last statement. "Manager? When did you become manager?"

Before I could speak up, and truly not knowing how to explain it, Gino jumped in. "When did he make you manager, Leo?

I held my hands up. "I had no clue until the detective told me. He showed me a ledger from Sal's book that he found on the desk. It had a change of my title in his books from security to manager dated two weeks ago."

I could tell Gino was thinking. His lips were pursed, and his eyes were looking up and to the right as if trying to remember something. "Sal must have done that just in case."

We all looked at him, puzzled, and Sara asked, "In case of what?"

Gino opened his mouth and closed it, clearly rethinking what he was originally going to say. "In case Sigaros needed a manager on the books for tax purposes."

Interrupting our conversation, the officers clapped their hands. "Okay, people, time to go. Detective Thomas wants everyone out of the area. We are conducting more of the investigation and want to ask Mr. Rossi if we could look around the building."

The answer Gino gave us didn't satisfy me, nor did it satisfy Sara from her look, but we all got up and headed for the door. Mike, Sara, and the twins were in their own conversation as we headed for the door. I could tell they were still talking about me being listed as the manager. Before we got too far, Gino grabbed my arm, and looking at the rest of the group in front of me, I held back and started to speak to Gino in a hushed voice. "I want to ask you some stuff about Sal. The detective was saying his past ill deeds and selfishness got him into this."

Gino darted his eyes around. In a firmer voice than I expected, he said, "Listen, Leo. I don't have to tell you, and it's not my place to say. That was Sal's business. I won't go into it." I could tell he wasn't going to budge.

Gino took my arm and, grabbing my hand, slapped a folded yellow piece of paper in it. "Here's Valentino's address." This time he had a little catch in his throat. "Sal would want to have him told in person. Not over the phone. Go tell him how... what... that Sal is dead. Please, Leo."

The way he said it, I didn't have the heart to say no to him. I nodded my head. He reached up and patted me on the side of the face with his hand.

"Okay, Gino. I'll go."

12

The two officers escorted us back to the police line. As we left, I reluctantly handed one of them my key to Sigaros. I pocketed the spare key just in case. Gino stayed back, awaiting Detective Thomas and the widening search of the murder scene. We could sense it between each other. There was a numbness that stayed with us. Turning to look back at the open front doors of Sigaros, I thought, *We'll never see Sal walk through those doors again.* Emptiness. That's all I could think of and feel next to the numbness. Sal filled that place, and it wouldn't be the same. Silently we just stood there for a while. Glancing over, I saw Kate holding Mia in her arms. I felt sad and angry to see Mia and Kate hurt so much. I could smell jasmine perfume wafting next to me. It felt nice in its own weird way to see Sara concerned. At least, I think she was concerned when she hit me and asked me where I'd been. Mike returned to that blank stare when I first met him today. He looked like a lost puppy.

Nudging my arm, Sara spoke up like a proud parent. "Sooo.... manager?" Her smile helped some of that numbness go away.

"Yeah, good job, Leo. I think you'd make a great manager," said Mia, finally with a little smile and a brightness in her eyes. "Maybe this means we won't have to look for another place to work."

"So, like, can you keep the place open?" Kate asked. There was no harshness to the question or judgment in its asking. It was more a question of whether I would be willing to take on the weight of keeping Sigaros open.

Wrinkling her nose, Sara spoke up. "Well, Leo just found out about being manager. Let's give him a minute to let it sink in." She saved me from what would have been a muddling explanation filled with protest and maybe acceptance. I don't know what being manager would even mean.

Instead, I closed my wide-open mouth and just nodded respectfully and said, "Thanks for the support, guys. It means a lot." Mike patted me on the back and smiled.

It was nice to see them all smile a little again. These were good people. My entire time at Sigaros, they had only ever been warm and friendly. Not like the folks at some of my old endeavors. I remember people there asking for superficial validation or, for some reason, becoming resentful or defensive, and we could never really work together. Here it was different. This was more my style. I think I want to see if I can reopen the place for them and for Sal.

I looked around at all of them and rubbed under my beard. "I don't know how to get Sigaros open again. Detective Thomas said it couldn't be opened until the case was closed."

"Not true," said Sara in an excited voice. "After all the forensic evidence is collected, regardless of the crime, a business can be reopened. I'm pretty sure I'm right. I'll check with one of my law professors."

"Sooooo, then Leo can keep the place open!" Mia and Kate said simultaneously with almost a squeal as they both wrapped their arms around me, squeezing me tighter than I thought possible. Not wanting to crush their enthusiasm, I rocked back and forth in their hug as my arms were trapped at my side. I grinned over at Sara and Mike.

Nodding my head slightly and in a crushed breath, I let out, "Well, let's see what Sara finds out."

Sara pulled them off, and I was so grateful for the hug, but to breathe again was so welcoming. Those ladies were stronger than they looked. Well, at least Mia was. Kate looked strong enough. The twins looked up at me and smiled.

A little sadness worked its way back into Mia's voice. "I'm glad it might be possible to open again. It won't be the same, though, not without Sal. Is anyone going to have a funeral for him?"

That energetic moment faded back to the reality of what had just happened. Sal was dead, reminding me that I needed to get to the church to talk to Sal's brother. I'm sure his brother would want a service. I bet Gino would want to do something too. "Let's just all go home and take a moment. I'll follow up with Gino to see if there's been anything planned after I go run an errand for him. I'll let you all know."

I reached out and gave the twins a hug and Mike a pat on the back, and they turned to go.

After they had gone a few paces, I turned to Sara. "Thanks, Sara."

Tilting her head a little, she said, "For what?"

Looking at my feet, I said, "For being here. For worrying. For being a... friend."

Her presence was comforting. It felt nice having her around. We stared into each other's eyes for a long moment. Then... whack! I got a slap to the meat of my chest. Not as hard as when I had first gotten there that day. I was more shocked than anything else.

"You answer your goddamn phone if I call you," she said through bared teeth ending in a grin. Pointing her finger up at me and with a raised eyebrow, she sternly said, "Got it?"

I smiled and rubbed my chest. It didn't really hurt, but as she'd gone through all the trouble to hit me, I'd feel bad if she didn't feel she'd accomplished something. Holding my hands up in acceptance, I said, "Fine! Fine." We both turned to leave, and while making my way to my bike, under my breath, I let out, "So violent." I could see her smile out of the corner of my eye.

Sara spun around, remembering, and with outstretched hands, said, "Oh! Hey. So, Sal had a brother?"

Shrugging my shoulders and with upturned palms, I said, "Yeah, I'm as surprised as you. I'm going to go let him know about Sal. I'll let you know how it goes."

We made plans to touch base later in the evening with an update about my meeting with Sal's brother and what she could find out from her professor. I checked my pocket and found the folded paper Gino gave me—Father Valentino Accardi, St. Jude's Cathedral, 702 Holy Cross Way, Las Vegas, Nevada 89109.

13

The weather had finally started to change. It was no longer hot enough to fry an egg on the sidewalk. Right around the beginning of November or sometimes just before Halloween, the temperature shifts in Vegas. The days become more tolerable—still hot, just not sweltering. The nights start to get cool. Not everyone knows how cold it gets in the desert at night or in the winter here, but I clearly recall that about every four years or so, it'll snow just enough to stick around for a few hours in the morning. Seeing a palm tree or the Flamingo Hotel and Casino sign with a light dusting of glistening snow is an oddity that never gets old.

The contrast of colors along the Red Rock Canyon shone brightly in the glow of the late afternoon sun, revealing the brilliance of the Mojave Desert. I still had about an hour before dusk, and I was well on my way. St. Jude's Cathedral is only about a mile and a half away from Sigaros. Besides still wrapping my head around the fact that Sal was dead, I was trying to grapple with the fact I was the one who was going to tell Father Valentino Arccadi that his brother was dead. If some guy showed up, who I'd never met or knew, and told me Gabe was dead, I think I'd punch him out. How was I going to even lead up to this conversation and have him trust that I even knew Sal? I think my internal monologue was showing. I noticed I was getting a wide berth from most of the passing drivers, and the looks or rather the side-eye glances of people trying not to look told me to stop muttering to myself and shaking yes or no to the internal questions running around in my head while I was biking.

Before I headed out, I decided not to incur Sara's wrath and miss a call by placing an earphone in one ear while biking. I was making good time.

With the weather cooling down, I took down my ponytail, and it felt nice to feel the cool breeze through my hair, and I was at a good enough pace to make my eyes squint from the wind. I used to have sunglasses, but every time I'd hit a pothole, I'd half fall off the bike, and the glasses kept flying off. I'd gone through about four pairs so far and had just given up. Mike even gave me a string tie for them once, and they still bounced off, and the string tie got twisted in my hair tie, and it was ridiculous getting it out. I wound up having Mia help me, and while she gladly helped, she left me in a French braid. Not that I can't pull off the French braid; it's just the upkeep. Too much work.

My internal monologue kept going, even with me trying to drown it out with the background noise of the local radio. I couldn't believe that Sal never spoke about his brother. Not that he had to, I guess, but stuff about family comes up. You eventually hear someone say something about a partner, cousin, parent, or sibling to someone. What else did Sal not say, and why wouldn't Gino go into Sal's past? Must be something a little dark… or not. I can't tell. Just then, the radio host talking in my ear had said the word "Sigaros" and now had my full attention.

"Breaking news. Owner of Sigaros bar and cigar lounge and well-known patron within the Las Vegas community was shot and killed today in the early morning hours. We have a clip from the lead detective who announced the murder just moments ago at a press conference. Here is what Detective Thomas has to say about the killing…"

A sense of panic struck me. All I could think of was *Oh great! Now Sal's brother is going to find out from a news bulletin. That's no way for someone to find out a family member was killed.* I throttled the electric bike to the limit feeling the buzz of the electric motor kick into a louder hum.

My attention was laser focused on the start of the broadcast. "Officers were called to Sigaros bar and cigar lounge this morning after receiving a report that a man's body was found inside. The victim, Mr. Salvatore Accardi, was pronounced dead at the scene. 'We have launched an investigation to establish the circumstances surrounding Mr. Salvatore Accardi's murder. We urge anyone with information about this crime to contact the local police station.'"

I need to make it there before Father Valentino finds out from the radio. I could see the spire of the church two blocks away as I heard Detective Thomas continue to give his announcement. Except this time, his delivery changed. It was almost accusatory, and he started the next part of the announcement with a scoff. My pulse immediately quickened at the memory of the last time I heard him do that.

"The murder has signs of prior Las Vegas mafia-connected murders dating back to the seventies. I'd also like to say that it is likely that Mr. Salvatore Accardi's own past associations with the mafia and prior indiscretions may have caught up with him and led to this incident and/or what may be a robbery gone wrong. We do not believe there is a wider risk to the community, and there will be an increased police presence in the area while carrying out the investigation."

The clip ended, and my adrenaline was surging. I was half a block away. My grip was ironclad, and I could feel my teeth grinding together and my triceps tighten as I leaned into the handlebars. The voice in my head was shouting. "How dare he insinuate that Sal had this coming and announce it publicly. Sal was a good man. He deserves to have someone who isn't jumping to conclusions. He deserves someone to not sully his name. He deserves someone to protect all that he's built at Sigaros and in the community."

I rounded the entrance to the church at full speed. A sense of accountability slapped me in the face. *If the detective wasn't going to be that someone, I would be. I would stand up and try to find the killer. I would protect all that he's done,* I said to myself and... it felt right.

Finding my constitution was invigorating. However, I was still at full speed, looking where to best enter the church, and completely missed the speed bump near the third set of olive trees lining the driveway. I launched straight up in the air, my momentum carrying me forward over the top of my handlebars, the pavement approaching faster and faster. I immediately heard my mother's voice tell me I'm going to crack my head open for not wearing a helmet. She was going to be so pissed if that happened, and I'd never hear the end of it. At the last moment, I tucked my head down and shifted to my left side. I slid on the asphalt for about five feet, scraping my left arm and leg as I did. I felt something crack along my chest and old scar tissue in my upper back made a loud pop. I came to a stop and rolled onto my back in the middle of the street. My breath was short, and I felt like I'd been kicked in the stomach by a horse. With my adrenaline up, I had enough sense to drag myself out of the street away from any oncoming cars to under the olive trees on the grass and just lay on my back.

14

It took me a good while to find my breath. I could barely relax out of the fetal position. I felt like I'd done a plank exercise for thirty minutes. I took in a deep breath. An immediate searing pain exploded over my left flank and stopped me short. I tried another less deep breath, and this time the pain was only mildly excruciating. "Yup, that's a rib."

I'd broken ribs before. Inevitably, in security work, you get into altercations and wind up in a tussle, and I'd had my share. Luckily my time in high school wrestling and some judo in college taught me how to take a hit and fall without breaking something more substantial like my neck. However, right now, it felt like all that prior experience was never going to prepare me to land well after being launched in the air on an electric bike while sliding five feet on the ground.

I needed to take stock of the rest of my body to see what did and did not work. Sitting there, I thought, *Okay, my fifth and or sixth ribs are likely broken. Let's try moving the legs. Please, oh please, let me be able to move my legs.* I'd seen guys take tumbles before and from the dumbest things wind up with neck injuries, not being able to walk again, and that scared the crap out of me. First, the right. I squeezed my eyes closed. I could move my foot and ankle and bend at the knee. Flexing the hip pulled on my lower back, but I could still move everything. *Phew*, and let out a breath. Okay, now the left. Same as the right, but I could feel a knot on my left thigh as I flexed my hip. It wasn't painful but I knew it was going to be sore from the fall on that side, and it wasn't as bad as I expected. *All right, that was a good start. Now let's try the upper body.* I moved my right arm and had no problems. *Okay, thank God, I'm out of the woods. Just the left arm.* I lifted my hand, then wrist and elbow, but as I got to my shoulder, a sting started to build. I crossed my left arm in front of me, and it felt like someone was scraping my arm with glass. I craned my neck, which luckily didn't explode in pain but still felt like a tight rubber band, and I looked down.

The left sleeve of my suit jacket and shirt was torn down to the elbow. I must have taken the brunt of the fall right there and not distributed the weight as well as I thought I did. Luckily my left leg took some of the impact. If it hadn't, I think the arm would have been broken instead of what looks like more bruised muscle with some significant road rash. I could see speckles of blood forming and dripping on the surrounding dress shirt. It wasn't anything out of a horror movie, but I was bloodied enough to warrant a decent first-aid dressing. Pieces of dirt and gravel speckled the arm.

With a pained breath, I let out, "That's gonna leave a good scar." I let my left arm fall slowly back to the coolness of the grass and winced. "Crap, that hurts."

I heard a crunching sound to my right. The crunch had the cadence of someone walking with hurried steps on the dried olive leaves and grass. I guess someone must have seen that tumble. The sound was almost right next to me. *I guess it's time to try and get up.* I hope getting up wasn't going to be as painful as I was expecting. I flexed my core and leaned onto my right side to try and meet the approaching footsteps. As I propped myself up with my right elbow, I noticed a warmth spread over my left eyebrow, and I had to blink my left eye a few times to wipe the wetness that was forming. I gingerly brought my left hand up to my eye and patted just above my eyebrow and felt a slight burning. I lowered my hand, and a deep scarlet stain covered my fingertips as though I had been fingerpainting.

With a sigh, I let out, "Great, my mother's never gonna let me hear the end of this," and shook my head.

The approaching crunching noise stopped. "You're probably right, son. A mother would be worried sick if she saw that fall, especially without a helmet."

The voice sounded familiar, very familiar. I turned and tilted my head up to look. Through a wet left eye and a good right eye, I could make out a tall figure of a man with salt-and-pepper hair with a Mediterranean complexion. I had to crane my neck a little more than expected to meet the man's face, given his height. A hand approached, followed by the feeling of an arm under my right side. Before I knew it, I was lifted gently to my feet. It takes a lot to lift a man of two hundred and fifty pounds who can't help along the way. Especially without having to pause to gain your balance in doing so. This guy lifted me in one even pull.

Finally standing upright, the man held my good shoulder and made sure I was balanced and let go. He was just about my height, but maybe a little smaller, and he looked… no, it couldn't be. I tried blinking a few times, not just because of the amount of blood in my eye, but I couldn't believe what I was seeing. It was Sal.

In a concerned and questioning tone, Sal asked, "Leo? Is that you?"

My mind started to race. I was shocked, or maybe in shock. I was so glad to see him alive. Why the charade? A sense of relief hit me. I let out a heartfelt sigh. "Oh man, Sal. Am I glad to see you. You had us all so worried. Mike and the twins are distraught, and Gino's… well, he's holding it together, but I can tell he's so upset." I held a hand out with my finger pointed at him. "Oh man! Sara is gonna be pissed letting us think you were dead."

The man took a white handkerchief out of his pocket and gingerly wiped the blood out of my eye. I finally had a good look. I was speechless. My heart sank, and the numbness I'd felt earlier in the day set back in.

The man rested a hand on my right shoulder and, in that same strong tone I'd come to hear from Sal, said, "Name's Father Valentino Accardi, son. I'm Sal's brother."

15

I stood there with a wide-open mouth struggling to find my next words, just staring at Father Accardi. A sinking feeling sat in, along with the numbness I previously felt. I finally let out an exasperated, "Sal's brother?"

Oh no, and I just told him his brother was dead. I'm such an idiot, and I closed my eyes for a second, regretting the last few moments in my life. In a hurried voice, I started to ramble. "Father Accardi, I am so sorry, sir. I was coming over to tell you about your brother Sal. I work over at Sigaros and have been there for the last six months. I didn't want to meet like this, Father, but I-I need to tell you what happened."

Just like before, he placed a hand on my shoulder and, in a calm voice, said, "Take a minute, Leo. You've had a bad fall. You're a little bit of a mess. Take a deep breath."

Wait. He called me Leo. I hadn't introduced myself yet. But he already knew my name. I took a deep breath and forgetting the cracked rib on my left side, felt that searing pain travel around from under my armpit to the middle of my back. I wound up with a small coughing fit and grasped my left side with each movement, and leaned over while still trying to intermittently hold the handkerchief over my left eyebrow.

After I regained my breath, I stood back up. I was finally able to ask one of the many questions now burning for an answer in my mind. Still squinting from the pain, I asked, "Father, how do you know me?"

"Sal and I talk frequently about you, Leo, as we do about his other friends at Sigaros. Sal comes to church here every Sunday to hear me give mass, and we spend the day catching up, mostly over a meal and a little wine in between a friendly card game of gin. He's described you well enough," and with a nod to the wreck in the street, said, "and your mode of transportation. Seeing a six-foot-three man in a suit with a reddish beard and long hair riding in on an electric bicycle narrows down who you are."

My head was starting to throb. I wasn't sure if it was from the fall, Sal's murder, or the fact that Sal talked about me, and with his brother for that matter. A little more sadness set in, knowing Sal took the time to include me as a friend. I noticed, too, that my pulse was starting to quicken as I remembered that someone had taken his life, shot him in the back, like a coward and that Detective Thomas was being a prick about working up the case and slandering Sal's name with insinuations. My fists started to clench. I took a shallower breath and tried to breathe the anger out of me. I was here to let Father Accardi know that his brother... my friend, is dead. I let my hands open.

"Father." I had to clear my throat so the words wouldn't start to catch in my throat as I knew they would. "I am so sorry. I came over to let you know Sal is dead. He was murdered sometime late last night."

Father Accardi looked down at his well-polished black leather shoes. He was dressed in a black shirt, pants, and jacket, with a white Roman collar identifying him to everyone as a priest. He had a similar build to Sal but maybe a little less stocky and just an inch or so smaller than me. He was clean-shaven and carried himself in that same tall stance that Sal did, looking like there was almost a rod down his back.

Looking back at me and meeting me eye to eye, he let out with sadness in his voice. "I know, Leo. I just heard on the radio."

My stomach turned. Had I been a little bit faster, I could have beaten Detective Thomas's announcement. No one should have to hear about a loved one that way. I didn't know what to say next.

I could feel my eyes starting to become glassy as I kept Father Accardi's gaze. "I'm so sorry, Father."

He stood by my left side and placed a strong supportive arm under it to support my weight until my left leg got moving and started to walk me toward the entrance of St. Jude's Cathedral. I let him guide me, and the first few steps took me a moment, and finally, my left leg woke up enough to support my weight, and the bruise that I knew was coming over my outer thigh hadn't begun just yet, and I was able to keep a fairly steady gait.

As we walked, Father Accardi spoke up in that same calm tone. "We'll go inside and get you cleaned up, and you can tell me what happened."

16

St. Jude's was a simple frame structure design, and its simplistic exterior was a stark contrast to its interior. My mother is Irish Catholic and follows the faith, but it never was my path. Don't get me wrong, I believe in something bigger than myself and that we are all connected somehow. I just never found my answers in organized religion. But walking into the grandeur of the church, I can understand the call. The cool light-beige marbled floor would have been a welcome relief in the hot Vegas weather, and the stained glass windows let in the morning and evening sun with a beautiful array of rainbows and light. The kaleidoscope effect bounced off the stark white walls. Behind the dais was an art deco painting of what could only be described as early man and woman with arms outstretched toward the cross. It gave one pause when one entered.

"Let's get you over to my quarters and clean you up a little," Father Accardi said, not betraying any sadness in his voice as he said it;

just a calm demeanor that I guessed came from his years as a priest. But from his walk, I could tell there was a somberness to his movements. I'm not sure Sal would have kept that calm had it been the other way around.

Father Accardi's quarters were on the second floor of the church. After walking a little, my left leg felt better and not tight like a rubber band. The heavy oak wooden door opened up to a modest living room with a beige cloth-covered sofa and matching armchair with the same heavy wooden coffee and side table as the door. There was a small kitchen against one wall behind it and a single door leading to a bedroom with an adjoined bathroom. It wasn't much, but it was quaint and welcoming. It had the same smell that Sal's office did. I thought I smelt cigar smoke lingering. The one commonality that I noticed between the office and Father Accardi's living quarters was a brick fireplace along one wall with the same design. I wondered if he had the same false drawer that Sal's did. The Father motioned me to his bathroom.

Walking in and closing the door, I got a good look at myself in the full-length mirror behind the door. My pants over my left knee had been ripped. My jacket was a shambles with a sleeve completely torn off from the left side as well as the underlying shirt. Taking a good look in the mirror above the sink, I saw that the scrape above my left eyebrow wasn't so bad. Head wounds have a tendency to bleed a lot and look worse than they are. I pressed around the lower part of my eye and just above the scrape, and it didn't hurt. I don't think I broke anything. I moved my jaw around to make sure there was no clicking and checked my teeth to make sure none were missing. All things considered, it wasn't the worst I'd ever looked. But it certainly wasn't the best. I splashed some cool water from the sink onto my face brushing away debris from the road that was lingering, and finally got a good look at the scrape. I'd have a good bruise and hopefully not too much of a scar above my left eyebrow, no more than half an inch of a cut that didn't need stitches. I put my hair back in a ponytail and slowly pulled off my jacket and shirt to look at my wounds on my left arm. I left my sleeveless undershirt on. It was more difficult than I thought to shimmy out of the jacket and torn shirt. I had to let my left arm dangle and let them fall off to the ground. Just as I did, I heard a knock on the bathroom door, and it was Father Accardi with new clothes and a first-aid bag in hand.

Motioning to the sink, he said, "Take a seat on the counter, Leo. I'll clean that up."

I complied. "You've done this kind of thing before, Father Accardi?" I said with a sideways quizzical glance.

"I used to do this for Sal back in the day."

I did a double take. So maybe Sal did have a bit of a rough-and-tumble past.

Father Accardi saw my look and carried on. "It's been some time, but you don't really forget."

He laid out the gauze and bandages, opened the bottle of hydrogen peroxide, and had a tube of bacitracin that he opened and applied to one of the clean gauzes. He raised a clean hand towel and the bottle of hydrogen peroxide.

"This won't hurt, Leo." Before he started, he looked me in the eye and, still in that calm tone, said, "Tell me what happened to Sal."

I had been dreading this moment, and I could feel myself starting to sweat and a sour taste formed in the back of my mouth. I kept his gaze and took a short breath. He started to clean up my arm. I looked forward and started to tell him what I knew. "Sal left Sigaros to run some errands yesterday and left me in charge. He telephoned around 9:00 p.m., saying he wanted the place closed at 10:00 p.m. sharp and that the poker game was going to start at 10:30. But I found out from Gino that Sal canceled the game."

Father Accardi stopped his methodical cleaning of my arm. I could see in his eyes that he was thinking, but also a small flash of anger was there, for only a moment and had I not been looking, I would have missed it.

"Is this Luigino? From Mickey's? Sal canceled the game?"

"Yes, Father, it is. Gino or Luigino said Sal canceled the game." I paused to see if there were any follow-up questions.

Father Accardi went back to dressing my arm and nodded for me to continue.

"Apparently, at about 10:45 last night, Sal asked Sara if the place was closed and that he was going to contact me." I turned to face him, and my voice came out a little more hurried than I expected. "But I didn't get any message."

He gently patted my shoulder. I looked down at my arm, and Father Accardi had done a nice job. The bandage covered the outer portion of my arm and was taped up well enough that any movement wouldn't cause it to immediately fall off.

Slapping his hands together, the Father said, "All right, now for the ribs. Take the undershirt off."

Father Accardi helped slip the shirt off over my head. He took out a large roll of medical tape. "Raise your arms up, and when I say, exhale all the way." He ripped the tape open and took a look at me, and said in a quick voice, "Okay, deep exhale."

I exhaled as much as I could, dreading the inhale that was to follow. He was quick. He definitely had done this before. Within fifteen seconds, he had wrapped tape around my torso three times. Just before I thought I was going to turn blue, he let out in a rushed voice. "Okay, breathe."

I was ready for that same searing pain to radiate through my chest and middle back, except this time, it was more of a dull ache. I couldn't expand my chest all the way given the taping, but I'll take that over the sharpness of the pain from before.

I smiled and looked over at him. "Thanks, Father Accardi."

He grinned back and handed me a new set of clothes he'd gotten from what I assumed was a donation box. There was a short-sleeved button-down black shirt. *Phew,* I thought. *This was going to be so much easier to put on than a T-shirt.* He then motioned for me to sit back down on the counter and began to prepare a smaller piece of gauze for my forehead.

I sat back down and, without him asking this time, went on with what I knew. "That was the last time anyone was known to speak to him. The rest of the information I got from Detective Thomas. He's the one who's taking over the case and the one who made the announcement over the radio." I could feel my pulse speed up a little and my back straighten up as I said the detective's name. "As per the detective, it seems like Sal had a few visitors just a little after messaging Sara. Maybe three, given the state of how turned over Sigaros looked." I stopped. Thinking about Sal alone possibly fighting off two or three guys was difficult to think about, but not as much as this next part. "Sal must have been shot first in the chest and then four times in the back."

I felt my vision starting to become glassy. I hadn't noticed that I was now standing with my fists clenched, but I knew my jaw felt tight.

I felt a hand over my fists. "Let it pass, Leo," Father Accardi said with a gentleness in his voice. I looked over and saw his eyes were glassy as well. He reached down to hand me a pair of light-gray sweatpants. "Put these on and come out to the living room. They should fit." He left and shut the door.

I placed my hands on the counter and bowed my head, sighing deeply. *This day absolutely sucks. I need to figure out who would have wanted to hurt Sal and why. I need to ask Father Accardi some questions.*

17

I finished putting on the sweatpants. They were a little loose around the waist and baggy throughout but at least the length was the right fit, and thankfully, they were easy to put on with one banged-up arm. I crossed over to the couch and joined Father Accardi, who was sitting on the armchair. He had a drink in his hand, and there was a second one waiting for me on the side table. He motioned for me to sit and drink. I sat and took a sip.

With wide eyes, I looked over at the Father and, in one exasperated word, said, "Gin?"

With a wink and a sip of his own drink, Father Accardi said, "See, Leo. Sal did talk about you." A small grin spread on his face. "Sal was a good man. A good older brother. We both are at an age where life starts to take more family and friends than it gives." Now with a little smirk, Father Accardi leaned forward, pointing his drink at me, and said, "Although, Sal had a knack for always making more friends. A trait I think you and he share."

I smiled back, raising my glass. "Thank you, Father."

He sat back in his chair. "Sal wasn't one to pick a fight." He paused, raising an eyebrow, and said, looking at me, "He would end them, though, if they got started. When we first moved here, he and I would get into a few scrapes, but he always came out on top. He saved my butt a few times. As much as our paths as youths eventually diverted, I never thought it would end like this for Sal." He dropped his head down a little and watched the ice clanging around in his glass. Without looking up, he said, "You know, he was the one who got me into the seminary. He was the one who made sure I stayed on the straight and narrow after our father passed away when we were teenagers. He always looked out for me...and others." Now looking back at me, setting his glass on the side table, "Even if the other person didn't ask to be looked after. He had a way of guiding people." Raising both hands and letting them fall on the armchair, he let out with a sigh, "He had his faults, as everyone does, and he had a rough few first years starting out on his own when I was away. He cleaned up his act when I finally got back to Vegas with a lot of hard work and some scrapes."

With that kind of a lead into their past, I figured now was as good a time to start asking some questions. I sat my drink down, "Father, I want to ask you a few questions." I raised my hands, showing my exasperation. "This... detective... made some innuendoes into Sal's past and, as I'm sure you heard from the radio, made it sound like Sal had connections to the mob and that this was the reason he was killed. I don't feel like Detective Thomas will go about solving Sal's murder without dragging his name and all the good he's done for others through the mud." I paused and sat up straighter. "Can you think of anyone that wanted to hurt Sal?"

The Father sat up in the chair, and adjusted his suit jacket, and looked at me a little puzzled. "I heard the detective and his insinuation, but I thought this was a robbery. Wasn't it?"

I looked straight at the Father and met his eyes, then shook my head. "It wasn't a robbery, Father. The detective let me know, and I figured out from some of the questions he asked, that the contents of the safe were all there even though it was open. The money from the evening's take wasn't removed from the security bag under the register. Sal hadn't even put his books away for the night. The detective handed me a paper from his ledger. I knew the design." I looked down, remembering the paper and Sal's handwriting and my surprise. Remembering the words next to my name made me feel a little warmer inside. But maybe that was the gin. "It had me listed as manager, actually," I said with a little chuckle.

Father Accardi sat back with his eyes looking to the ceiling, put his hands together, mouthed a silent prayer, and made the sign of the cross. I waited silently, looking at the fireplace. Father Accardi rose. I shifted in my seat to stand, and he motioned for me to sit. "I need to make a phone call. Wait here."

He went toward the kitchen, where there was a landline phone hanging on the wall. He reached into his inside jacket pocket and pulled out a little black notebook and tortoiseshell reading glasses. I watched and waited as he thumbed through the pages and dialed a number.

With the receiver on his shoulder, he turned back to the couch, looking at me over the glasses. "Gino said Sal canceled the poker game last night?"

I replied with a quick. "Yes, Father."

Father Accardi lifted his chin in acceptance.

The person he called picked up on the second ring. "John? It's Father Val."

There was a pause as the person on the other line spoke. Father Accardi removed his reading glasses and looked to the ground, nodding as he listened.

"Thank you, John. It's a loss to us all. Sal was a good man and a good friend. I'll work on having something arranged. I needed to ask you. I know you're a regular at the Monday night poker game. Did Sal cancel last night?" The Father looked back down to the ground, nodding. "Thank you again, John. I'll ring you as soon as I have information on a service for Sal."

He hung up the receiver with a heavy thud and stood looking at it, and without turning to me, said, "Sal did cancel the game. That was John. He's a friend of Sal's and is in one of the offices across from Sigaros." He let his hand drop to his side and sighed. Quietly he made his way back over to the armchair and sat back down.

I didn't speak. I just let him be. Why did he call John? Why didn't he believe me when I told him that Gino said Sal canceled the game? Maybe he didn't trust me.

I cleared my throat a little and spoke up. "Father Accardi, sir. I know we've just met, but I wouldn't have lied to you about Sal canceling the poker game."

The Father smiled at me, held one hand up, and let it fall to the armchair. "I'm sorry, Leo. It's not you that I didn't believe." He sighed. "It's Gino."

I was a little taken aback. I knew Gino said Val and he didn't exactly get along, but I was surprised he wouldn't take his word about Sal canceling the game.

Before I had a chance to ask, the Father spoke up. "Gino, Sal, and I go way back. Back to when Sal and I moved here with our father in 1950." He paused, choosing his words. "Gino and I have had a few disagreements, and in our earlier lives, I found his character questionable at best. Sal never did. He always considered him a friend even with some of the things that happened."

Just as the Father finished, my phone rang, which surprisingly survived my spectacular crash. I reached into my right pocket to try and silence it and saw that it was Sara. A little chill ran down my back. I needed to answer this call, or I'd never hear the end of it.

I held the phone and, with my best pleading look, I turned to Father Accardi. "Father, I apologize. This is Sara. If I don't answer, she will literally pour salt on my wounds. Do you mind?"

Father Accardi grinned. He and Sal really did look quite similar. "Sal told me about her fire. You'd better answer it."

I silently mouthed, "Thank you," stood and moved to the kitchen, leaving Father Accardi to his thoughts. I saw him pick up his drink and take it all down, and I answered the phone.

Sara answered in a sarcastic tone. "Good. You value your life."

I shook my head. "Nice to hear from you too, Sara. What's up?"

In a quick and hurried voice, she said, "I spoke to my professor, and I need to talk to you to see what we can do about opening Sigaros. It looks like it may be possible, but I need to know what the ledger said and what the detective told you. Let's meet at the coffee shop next to Sigaros."

"Sara, I'd be happy to meet you and talk, but I'm with Father Accardi, Sal's brother..." I smiled, looking back over my shoulder "...and I haven't finished."

In a whispered, apologetic tone, she let out, "Oh! Sorry, Leo." That tone didn't last long. She was back to the hurried voice she started out with. "I have to get going. I'm double-parked. I still need to talk in person to see if I can move things along to open Sigaros."

I tried to pace my voice to see if I could have her match mine to have a less rushed conversation. "Okay... but I need to go home and change first."

She paused and dryly asked, "Why?" I could just see her on the other side of the phone with her hand on her hips. Her tone changed to a more inquisitive nature. "What happened?"

I really didn't feel like letting her know. Protesting, I said, "Nothing... I... just need to, that's all."

With a puff from the other end of the phone, she said, "Okay, fine. I'll meet you at your parents' house in thirty minutes. That should give you enough time to pay your respects to Sal's brother. You need to tell me about him. I'm so curious."

In a hushed quick voice, I answered, "No! Just give me a minute to change, and I can meet you wherever."

With a placating tone, she said, "Oh, it's fine. It'll be quicker this way. I need the info now, and I may need to get to a notary after I see you, and there is one near your parents' house that's open until seven."

"NO! Sara!" I tried to protest, but she'd hung up before I had the chance.

I let my head fall and turned back to Father Accardi, who was already standing.

With a grin, he said, "Best do what the lady asks, son."

"I'm sorry, Father Accardi. I really wanted to ask you a few things, but I need to go."

He held up his hands and made his way to his front door. "Come here for dinner tomorrow. You can help make the gravy for the pasta, and we will see about your questions. I have to make a few calls and arrangements for Sal." His last statement was said in a somber tone.

I nodded and headed to the door. I stopped before I left and turned and faced him.

"Father Accardi." I looked him in the eyes. "I'm so sorry for your loss. I want to do right by Sal, and I want to find out why this happened."

He stuck out his hand, and I shook it. As I did, he grasped mine with his other hand and said, "I'm sorry for your loss too." He gave me a small smile. I could tell he was in pain from Sal's death, and the realization that he was murdered for something more than a robbery was starting to weigh heavy in his thoughts. He let go, held up a wide open hand, and looked at me. "Five o'clock tomorrow. The gravy will take about an hour and a half to make."

I smiled back. "Yes, Father Accardi."

With a grin, he patted me on the back and opened the door. "Call me Val. Be safe, Leo."

With a wave of my right hand, I saluted goodbye. "Thanks, Val."

18

The glow of the neon signs was already brightening the night skyline with beautiful arrays of fluorescence. I found my bicycle where I'd left it, under the olive trees. Reaching down to pick it up, I had to keep my left hand on my sweatpants to keep them from falling. *I really don't want Sara or my mother to see me looking like this.* Each time I moved, I expected a radiating pain around my chest from my cracked rib. However, the taping Val gave me helped tremendously with any exertion.

After my fall, I had remembered to take stock of my injuries but neglected to give the bike a once-over. It was an older road bike to begin with that was retrofitted with an electric motor and showed its miles but got the job done. The chain was completely broken. It looked like the bracket holding the electric motor was hopefully just loose, and the handlebars were off-center. With a sigh, I straddled the bike. My left leg felt tight, but I still had full range of motion without feeling a hitch as I swung it over. Reaching down with both arms this time, I flexed to pull the handlebars back to center. I felt the strain in my left arm, and it burned like something crazy, but the muscles responded and still had their strength. I was able to pull the bars back to about ten degrees off-center. *So far, so good. Now for the moment of truth.* Bending over, I shoved the battery back in its bracket and shifted it back into place. My only shot of getting home, given the absent chain, was to see if the electric motor still worked with the throttle. Closing my eyes, I whispered a quick succession of "Please, please, please."

There was a low hum, and the bike lurched forward in the gear I was in before the crash. I was off! It was a fight most of the way home. I had to keep both hands on the bars to force them to keep straight, and it seemed as though the front brakes were the only ones working. At my first stoplight, I almost fell over the front of the bike. Luckily, I had throttled down and was only creeping forward.

I rounded the corner to my parents' house, glancing down at my watch. I had made it with five minutes to spare. Usually, there weren't any cars parked out front. For whatever reason, tonight, there were two. There was an open-air jeep and what looked like a Honda Civic.

A small wave of frustration hit me. *Why, oh, why was Sara early, and why, oh, why was my brother back over at the house?* I slowly came to a stop in front of both cars. Maybe they were still in their cars. No such luck. I brought the bike to the side of the house.

Maybe they'd be near the front entrance, and I could sneak upstairs quickly. With pursed lips, I took out my keys, grasped the door-knob, and in slow motion, inserted my keys, turned the lock, and wedged the door open to poke my head inside.

It seems everyone, and I mean everyone, was right there sitting at the kitchen table. Sara was sitting in between my mother and Gabe and across from my father. I hung my head. *Well, no way around this.* Stepping through the door, they all turned. Each person's conversation immediately halted, and I was greeted with questioning brows and wide-open mouths.

Holding up my hands, hoping to hold off the onslaught of coming questions, I tried to answer for my appearance, "I can ex—"

I could see my mother look at my forehead and immediately place a hand on her hip and start to raise her hand.

But before I could get the word "explain" out, Sara spoke up, shaking her head with her finger already pointed at me. "Let me guess. You finally crashed that bike, and without the helmet I told you so many times to wear? Leo, come on, you know better. Luckily you don't look worse than when you started."

My mother surprisingly put her finger down, having nodded along with all of Sara's statements, and then just shook her head with clasped hands covering her heart. "Why will you not listen to people who have your best interests at heart? Are you okay? Did you hurt anything else? Where did you get those clothes? Why are you sneaking in the side door?"

All the while, my brother was sitting there grinning. "Yeah, Leo, why won't you just listen to people who have your best interests at heart? I like the pants."

Trying to interject, I finally was able to get out, "Thank you. I did have a little tumble, yes, and I'm fine." Conceding, I pointed to my mother and Sara with an open hand. "Ma, Sara, you are both correct. I should have worn a helmet. As for the clothes, a priest gave them to me. He was also the one that bandaged my head. By the way, everyone, this is Sara. Sara, this is Ma, Dad, and Gabe."

In unison, they all said dryly, "We've met."

My father was looking me over with concern. He was always good about not giving me too hard a time if he knew I had a rough day, even for all his lectures on what I should be doing in my life.

"This nice young lady said she is a coworker of yours and that you two need to go over some last-minute contracts for work. That is since you became manager?" He stood and looked up at me—he was a good six inches shorter—and patted me on both shoulders. "I'm glad you're okay. I wish you would have told us you'd become manager. We're all so proud of you, Leo." To my surprise, he gave me a quick hug.

That stopped all the comments about my appearance, or where I'd been, or why I was sneaking in the side door. The look on my mother's face had turned to joy instead of one of concern. My brother was still sitting there stupidly grinning, and Sara just mouthed an "awe" to me.

My father saved the moment yet again, saying, "Go get cleaned up and help this young lady."

"Thanks, Dad," I said, a little stunned and confused. "The manager job just happened, and it's just until I can see about my other projects."

My father, now looking at me, said, "Still, I'm glad you're putting in the work." He left to refill his coffee cup.

Turning to go to the staircase, I said, "Sara, I'll be ten minutes."

With a smile this time, Sara said, "No rush. Your mother and Gabe were just telling me a few stories about your prior escapades."

To that, I replied, "I'll be five minutes."

I jogged off to the stairs, hearing my brother behind me in a little sarcastic tone, "Take your time."

As quickly as I could, I put a brush through my hair and put it back into a ponytail, splashed some water over my face, and took off the donated clothes; exchanging them for a pair of dark jeans and a dark button-down shirt that was easy to put on and wouldn't show any incidental scrapes if they happened to bleed through. All the taping and bandages were holding nicely and hadn't bled through. This really wasn't Val's first time patching someone up.

I grabbed a jacket and headed down. I was still trying to figure out why Gabe was here, but that question was answered halfway down the stairs. My mother had again enlisted his help in setting up decorations. Not only his help, but it seemed Sara was pitching in and was deep in conversation with Gabe as I reached the first floor.

Not seeing my mother around, I yelled out, "Ma, why are you having Sara put up Christmas decorations? I thought we were all done?"

From our storage closet, she answered, "Because the nice young lady offered, Leo. I found three more boxes after last time. Gabe, come and grab the last one. Leo, help Sara put the Christmas village on the top shelf."

Gabe turned to me. "Sara, I'll finish the story later. Coming, Ma."

I shook my head. "What story, Gabe?" He just smiled. With raised eyebrows as much as I could with the tape still above my left eyebrow, I asked again a little louder, "What story, Gabe?" He just walked off.

I went over to Sara, who was on a step stool, and she motioned for me to hand her the last Christmas village. Handing it to her, I asked in a low voice through gritted teeth, "Why didn't you wait outside?"

She placed the village up on the shelf, plugged in the lighting for the small house, and turned it on. She was just about eye level with me, maybe an inch above in those boots.

"And how was I supposed to know you weren't already here?" She reached her hand out for me to help her down, and I grabbed it and shook my head. "I rang the door, and Gabe answered. I explained who I was and why I'd come, and he graciously asked me to come in. Then he introduced me to your mother and father, who I might add were very happy to hear about how much hard work you had put in at Sigaros and that you're acting manager."

A little exasperated, I said, "Why'd you tell them that?"

"Because, like it or not, Leo, you are acting manager." I let that sink in a little. "Come on. We have to get going. The notary closes at seven, and we need to have you sign your employment contract showing you've accepted the position of manager."

I was confused. "What are you talking about?"

Grabbing her jacket from the side table, she said, "I'll explain as we go, and you can explain to me what happened to you and how things went with Sal's brother."

I yelled out, "Ma, Sara and I have to go. I'll be back later tonight."

My mother came out to the door with Gabe and my father poking their heads around the corner. Ma came over and gave Sara a big hug. "Thanks for coming over, dear, and for the help. It was so nice to meet you." She leaned in, whispering enough for me to hear, "He never brings any of his friends over, let alone a woman." I could see Sara grinning.

I rolled my eyes and grabbed Sara by the arm, motioning to the door. "Thanks, Ma." I gave my mother a quick hug and a peck on the head.

Waving to everyone, Sara said, "It was nice to meet you all." Arching her neck to look at my brother, she said, "Gabe, you have to tell me the rest of the story."

Gabe raised a thumbs-up, and my parents both said, "So nice to meet you too. Come back anytime." With that, I hurried Sara out the door down to the jeep.

19

The coolness of the desert November air was refreshing in the open-air jeep. I was glad to have gotten out of my parents' house and to have brought my jacket along.

Sara didn't waste any time and got right to the point. "Sooo... I have a way we can keep Sigaros open. I met with one of my professors, and they said it was possible to keep a business open, even with a crime under active investigation, if there was an acting manager to run the place. Which, from what you've told me from Sal's ledger, is you."

She seemed so proud of herself.

"I don't know, Sara. That seems a bit of a stretch. I mean, I never signed a contract or an employment agreement stating I was going to be manager, and we only have Sal's ledger saying I was named in the position."

"Correct, but that's considered a proof of change in position, given that it's in the business's financial records. Sal had me help him with his employment contracts a few years ago, and there is a clause in there stating that amendments to the job description and title can be made at the discretion of the employer. All we have to do is have you sign the additional section of the addendum of your contract stating you accept the position of manager. We also have corroborating proof from a separate business owner, Gino, stating that Sal made you manager."

My skepticism must have still been showing because she said, "Come on, Leo. It's the best we've got to try and keep the place open." She followed it with a good-natured slug to my left arm.

Now being hit by Sara previously, I know that she could drive a punch home, but this was a nice little tap. Regardless, it sent a staggering electrical pain from my bandaged triceps up to my neck. I inadvertently took a deep breath, forgetting about my cracked rib. The taping Val had done was holding up, but the combination of the pain over my arm and my ribs made me have to hold my breath for a good ten seconds. I had to let the pain pass and bowed my head, grazing the front dash with my right hand, leaving an indentation.

Looking back and forth between the road and me, Sara let out, "What the hell happened, Leo? You took worse of a fall than you told us, didn't you? Why didn't you say something?"

The throbbing pain was passing and becoming a dull ache, and I could breathe again. "I was headed over to see Father Accardi—

Val—and as I was coming up to the church, I missed a bump and launched off my bike. My left arm took the brunt of the fall. I cracked at least one rib on that side, my clothes were trashed, and I'm pretty sure I'm gonna have a bruise down my entire outer left thigh tomorrow, but hopefully not too much of a scar from the scrape above my left eye."

Sara stopped short at an upcoming yellow light and turned to me. "Holy crap, Leo! Do we need to get you to a hospital?"

I waved her off. "No, no. Val patched me up pretty well. He saw me take the tumble and brought me into the church, cleaned me up, and gave me some new clothes." I paused. "While he was cleaning me up, I told him about Sal." I still couldn't believe Sal was gone. It didn't feel real.

The light turned green, and a short honk sounded behind us, and Sara took off. We didn't speak for the next two lights.

"How'd Val take it? What's he like? Wait, Val? Shouldn't we call him Father Accardi?"

I turned to her, grinning. "Val told me to call him that. I guess he felt comfortable enough. I think you still have to call him Father Accardi."

Sara saw the grin. "I swear, you and Sal can make friends faster than anyone I know."

Still grinning, I said, "True. It's one of my many gifts."

Rolling her eyes, she said, "Shut up, Leo. So, how'd Father Accardi take it?"

"He's a lot like Sal. They look similar. Val's a little trimmer and shorter, but not by much, and has stark white hair. I think… I think he took it as well as anyone can take that kind of news. He was calm and, of course, sad about it. Oddly enough, though, he did question one or two things that I told him, especially about Gino. Sounded like Gino and him have a little history."

"Like what?"

"Not sure, really. I'm going over tomorrow night for dinner at the church and was going to ask a little more about that and Val and Sal's earlier days in Vegas and see if he could think of anyone that wanted to hurt Sal."

"Why didn't you ask him while you were there tonight?"

"Gee, let me see. Because I took a wicked fall and because you called me and told me to come right away, that's why."

"All right, all right, fine. Thank you for answering your phone and for coming. Don't get all uppity." With a more serious tone, she asked, " But don't you think Detective Thomas is going to do that?"

My next statement came out a little harder than I anticipated. "NO. That guy's a prick. He's already made up his mind about Sal. Detective Thomas won't hesitate to drag Sal's name through the mud before this is over. I'm damn sure not gonna let that happen."

Sara was quiet as we pulled up to the notary office and turned the engine off. In a calm voice, she said, "Okay, Leo. Just... just be careful. Whoever killed Sal probably knows you too. They probably know all of us at Sigaros. If they did target Sal, and if it wasn't a random murder, don't get caught off guard. Not everyone you meet is going to be your friend, Leo."

I turned, and we stared, just looking into each other's eyes. I leaned in, grinned, and with my most suave voice, said, "Why, Sara, with everyone being a friend, it's hard to have enemies." I winked. "Remember, it's one of my gifts." I patted the dash with my right hand and popped out of the jeep. "Come on, let's get this signed. I want to get some rest."

20

It was good to be back. The vibrance of the city was palpable the moment you came north on the freeway. The desolation of the desert was endless, but as soon as you crossed over that last ridge, the lights of Vegas felt like a welcoming beacon. This city had it all. Gambling, prostitution, drugs, money laundering. There was so much money and, more importantly, power. Everything was always so ripe for the taking. I'd been gone too long.

The flight from Cleveland to Los Angeles was never so exhilarating. Finally, those old capos were dead. They'd been so fond of Salvatore. Made me want to spit. I'm no longer held to their demands. At least for now. It's time. I've a score to settle with this town. It owes me a lifetime of payback, and I know just where to start. Coming in through L.A., no one'll even know I've arrived until everything's set in motion.

That drive into Vegas felt like the last thirty-five years. Cleveland was no Vegas. Sure there was business to be had, but not like here. As soon as I saw the glow of the neon lights, I could sense myself starting to salivate. I'd been a starving man, lost on old men and their plans, their ideas, their desires, all this time. Now I could drink from my own well and indulge without restraint.

Given the rackets back home in Cleveland, I'd collected a pocket full of easy debts to call on from all over the country. It was easy to pick up muscle from L.A. All I needed was three or four guys, anyways. He was older now. He'd have lost a step or two. I probably wouldn't even need them to get rough with him. Sal's been out of the game so long he's gotten soft. Not me, though. I still wanted it all and more. I want this town. I could pick up a larger crew when I got into town with any other debts owed me.

I bet Sal still knew all the good places in town to hit and where to begin. He always kept a record in that little book of his. This town was still open for business and had grown weak from my absence. At least, that's what the old crew and current family and informants in town let on to the bosses before they passed. No one will know what's hit them when I start back in. All I need is a single base of operation. A foot in the door. Nothing more.

He'd taken care of the bosses so well they'd given him a free pass and let him open his own place without interference and even let that little prick Gino go with him. I'll take it all from him and Gino. Sal will watch his beloved Sigaros and Vegas turn into my dream.

That book of his will just be the beginning. It'll be mine. No one will stop me this time.

I can't wait to see my good friend Sal.

21

We'd arrived at the notary with only a few minutes to spare. The person behind the counter wasn't too keen on helping us so close to closing. However, after Sara started, that changed. It's always interesting to see Sara work. She doesn't use her attractiveness for manipulation, although she definitely could; rather, she's practical, straightforward, and has the innate ability to remind people of the value of their job and doing it well. Something Sal was good at too. We were in and out in less than ten minutes with a document signed and notarized stating that I had accepted the job as manager of Sigaros. Had you told me six months ago that I would be manager of a place I just went to have a good drinking cigar at, let alone looking for the owner's murderer, I would have called you crazy, but here we are.

Walking out of the notary into the comfortable coolness of the early evening, I turned to Sara and said, "Sara, thank you. I know

Sal would've wanted the place to keep going. I hope this does the trick."

Sara said, "Sigaros really is as much our place as it was Sal's. I'm doing this for all of us." She turned and looked at me. "I think you need this place too. I'll give you a ride back to your parents' place."

We started back to my home when I remembered something she mentioned while we were waiting at Mickey's to talk with the detective. "Hey, I forgot to ask. Did you ever figure out who that person with the raspy voice was who called Sal?"

"No, I never did. All I could tell was he was probably around the same age as Sal, the way he emphasized that he 'Wanted to talk to his good friend Sal.'"

Something didn't sit right with me. Not that I knew all of Sal's old friends. But I knew a good many of the regulars who came through either for cigars, drinks, or poker games. I would have remembered somebody with a raspy voice.

"Let me see if Gino knows anybody like that. I have to give him a call and let him know I spoke to Val anyways."

I dialed Mickey's and got the barman Richie and asked to speak to Gino.

"Bonasera, Leo, how'd things go with Valentino?"

"It went okay. He was appreciative, I think, of someone coming over to tell him about Sal. Hey Gino, I'm trying to figure out a few things that happened before... Sal got murdered. I was chatting with Sara, and she mentioned that before he went out that day, he got a phone call from an old friend with a raspy voice asking to talk to his 'good friend Sal.' I don't know anybody like that. Would you?"

Gino didn't answer, and there was a long silence.

I said, "Gino, you there? Did I lose you?"

Gino answered very calmly. "You say a man with a raspy voice called saying he wanted to talk to his 'good friend Sal'?"

"Yeah. Sara was pretty specific about him saying 'good friend.' Why? Do you know the guy?"

In a dry voice, Gino said, "Come to the restaurant. We need to talk." He hung up.

I looked at the phone. *What was that about?*

I turned to Sara. "Hey, you mind dropping me at Mickey's? Gino said he wanted to talk. Or rather, told me to go over now."

Sara said, "Sure, it's not too far. He told you to go over?"

"Yeah, he didn't ask. It was definitely an order. Maybe he's just stressed about everything. But hopefully, he can tell me something about that guy."

Sara got me to Mickey's within a few minutes. Getting out of the jeep, she stopped me and made me look at her. "Remember what I said. Be careful."

I could tell she was worried. I decided not to try and be smart with my response. "You got it. Let me know how things go with submitting the paperwork."

Turning the jeep back on, she said, "Will do. I should have news by tomorrow if we can reopen once I submit this to the police. You do the same. Let me know how things go with Gino..." She finished with a little bit of a sarcastic tone, "... and Father Accardi," and stuck her tongue out at me as she left.

22

I tightened my ponytail and walked through the double doors of Mickey's. Even with the recent news of the murder next door, the restaurant was packed, although that may have drawn out some of the crowd. Mickey's was a classy place, and the clientele included businessmen, lawyers, doctors, high rollers in town and from out of town, and locals who had been coming here for the last thirty years. Gino always made the place feel welcoming, just like Sal.

As I entered, I looked over to the piano bar. I looked to my far left, where Gino was usually standing to survey the place, but instead, I found the barman Richie. I got the nod from him as he was cleaning glasses to head to the very back of the house. I turned my gaze and saw Gino at the farthest corner of the restaurant, sitting at a table by himself with a single candlelight barely illuminating the table. I nodded back and made my way through the restaurant. The place was hopping, and I could hear conversations mostly directed at this morning's recent events.

There was a very fat obnoxious sounding man, who I assumed to be a lawyer, talking loudly. It was hard not to overhear him. As I passed by, I heard him say, "Yeah, that guy Sal next door probably got what he had coming. Those old guys are all part of that old mob crew. If they didn't die out long ago they should be wiped out now. I bet that guy was still shaking down folks and running a racket, and that's probably why he got popped."

Those words stopped me in my tracks right next to the man's shoulder. He had a few other people with him, three men and two women who all looked to be lawyers but younger. My pulse started to quicken, and I could feel my shoulders tighten. I turned to face the table and looked down at the man who had made the remark about Sal.

The steel in my voice carried across to the surrounding tables and garnished most of their looks. "Mr. Salvatore Accardi was a good man and not involved in ANY racket. You'd do well to be respectful of his name and his memory."

The lawyer laughed and started to stand up. "And what the hell are you gonna do if I say anything else about hi—?"

Before he ended his sentence, I had a hand on his shoulder with my left fist clenched. He was pudgy with no muscle on him. I could tell by the way I grabbed his shoulder that he wasn't ever accustomed to physical work, let alone a fight. With my blood up, he wasn't going to make it past his next syllable. With my right hand, I set the fat lawyer back down in his chair without any effort. I stood leaning in over him. The rest of his table had stopped smiling as well as the obnoxious man. He started to cower, and I could see the fear of the oncoming punch setting in, and he started to raise his hands in defense. Before I could even raise my left hand, Gino was on my left, and Richie was on my right.

Gino grabbed my left hand, and Richie placed an arm under my right bicep. They wouldn't have stopped me from pummeling this guy. Not that Gino or Richie couldn't handle themselves. But I was better than both of them in a fight and would have pushed straight through them. I stopped because it was Gino. Had it been anyone else, I wouldn't have thought twice.

Gino spoke up like a gracious host. "I see you've met the new manager of Sigaros next door. This is Leo. Leo, this is the assistant district attorney Mr. Richards."

I kept looking down at the now pale lawyer. I kept my eyes on him. Between gritted teeth, I told Gino, "He was talking shit about Sal. I won't have anyone saying that he got what he had coming."

Without pause, Gino looked over at the man and said politely, "I'm sure Mr. Richards would never insinuate that my dearest and oldest friend Sal had been murdered because he had it coming." He paused then and looked over the table. "Because I'm sure he would never be that disrespectful to my friend or to me. Let alone have to be reminded how many times I've made sure that his son, no matter how drunk he was, never left here in his own car." Now looking back at the fat obnoxious lawyer, he finished with a more steeled tone. "Because if he did, I'd have no objection to Leo beating the absolute shit out of him in front of the entire professional Vegas community for the level of disrespect he presumed to offer to me, Sal, Leo, and this establishment."

The patrons at the tables surrounding us all stopped their conversations. The man just nodded. Gino smiled and said, "Good. Richie, see that the next round of drinks are on the house for the table."

Richie nodded and let loose my arm. Gino pulled me away. I was still staring at the man.

Gino had to raise his voice, "Leo! Let it go."

He walked me back to his table in the corner, waved to Richie at the bar, raised two fingers, and pointed to the table. We sat down, and I was still looking back at the table.

"I'm sorry, Gino. I didn't mean to upset your restaurant. I meant no disrespect. But I won't have someone saying those things about Sal."

Gino waved a hand. "I'm glad you said something, Leo. It's inevitable that people will talk, and I would want friends of Sal's to remind people that he was a good man. Everyone has a past and prior recklessness in their youth. It shouldn't dictate how they are remembered." This time he pointed a finger at me, following up with, "But there's a way to say it. You can't let your anger get in the way. You have a responsibility to Sigaros now and your employees. You represent Sal, Sigaros, and its values."

He finished the drink he had on the table and stared down at the ice cubes.

Gino's words left me with more questions than I came in with. "Gino, this Detective Thomas. It seems as though he's already made up his mind about this being related to a mafia issue from his past. I want to figure out what happened without having Sal's life slandered. I want to know a few things about his past."

Richie had come back around and placed two fresh drinks in front of us. Gino lifted his glass and sipped. I left mine on the table.

Gino looked up at me and said, "Yeah, I get the same feeling about that detective. But first, how'd things go with Valentino? Did he hit you in the forehead or something?"

I placed both hands on the table and, with a deep breath, said, "Things went as well as could be expected. I took a tumble and wrecked the bike. Val patched me up, and I told him about Sal. I'm headed back there tomorrow for dinner."

Gino choked a little on his drink. "Val? He asked you to call him Val?"

"Yeah. Why?"

"He has only ever let a few people call him Val. I am not one of them. I knew him before he was Father Accardi, and he barely let me call him Valentino after what happened years ago."

"Gino, you have to give me a clue here. What happened? What were you, Val, and Sal up to years ago, and why is it all so veiled? Do you know who the guy with the raspy voice is who called Sal? I want to get to the bottom of Sal's murder and clear things up. You gotta help me."

He held up his hands again. "Fine, fine. I don't like talking about other people's pasts unless I get their okay, but given the circumstances and where things are at, I guess I can tell you what I know."

He took a long sip of his drink. I still didn't touch mine. He sat back and waved for Richie to come over.

"I first met Sal when we were both seventeen. His dad was a contractor and mason worker for the Desert Inn and the Sahara Hotel. Sal and Valentino worked with their dad at different job sites. After Sal's dad passed early in 1960, he started working at the Sahara Hotel off what was San Francisco Street before it became the Sahara and the El Rancho Hotel downtown as a busboy and was occasionally working at the Las Vegas International Golf and Tennis Club. I'd come out from Cleveland on my own and started working for one of the Cleveland families running numbers and happened to frequent all three establishments for the family. Sal was trying hard to take care of his brother Valentino who was fourteen at the time. It was rough on Sal. Given that he wasn't eighteen, he wasn't legally able to take over care of his brother, and they were about to be separated."

Richie came over.

Gino said, "Bring us over four appetizers and bring my ledger from my office."

Gino saw my wide-eyed expression.

"Yes, I worked for one of the Cleveland families under Frank Milano and eventually under the Genoveses. Like I said, everyone has a past and prior indiscretions. Those indiscretions in one's youth shouldn't dictate how they are perceived." He took a drink. "Sal and I ran into each other one night after a few people were working me over, and he saved my ass." Gino chuckled. "He took down the two of them with a combination punch, and the third guy just ran. Sal was something."

Richie came out with a platter of appetizer and the black ledger. Gino motioned for me to dig in. I was famished and wasn't going to refuse.

Gino placed both hands on the closed ledger and said, "Sal and I got to be close friends. He told me about his troubles and about how he learned the trade of mason work from his father and wanted a job to help support himself and his brother. I asked my lieutenant at the time to help out and he gave Sal a job at riding protection for our tucking business. Sal did well. He had a little bit of pent-up anger after his dad died, and I think it let him work out his frustration when the situations came about to flex his strength, but that was short-lived. Sal never wanted to hurt anyone. He eventually wound up being able to talk his way through any confrontation.

He was making good money and was able to take care of his brother. Being that he was connected now with the Cleveland family, the law left him alone, and within six months—by the time he was eighteen—he was Valentino's legal guardian. Sal came to me a few months later and asked to be taken off protection and placed on something else. At the time, I was looking to expand my interests beyond numbers to make enough to maybe buy my way out of the lifestyle. The longevity of a mobster is nothing to count on. There was a young up-and-comer within the family that had been sent out to work on expanding operations. He was a slick, thin guy with a raspy voice named Franco Verga. Franco was working on money laundering, robberies, shakedowns, and dabbled in arson. He wanted to have his hands in everything, and Vegas was like an amusement park to him. He was looking for more help, so Sal and I went to work for him. Franco was smart but vindictive. He tended to fly off the handle. There was a story that was going to run about him in the Las Vegas Sun late in November 1963. The newspaper's offices mysteriously burned down that month."

Gino paused and took another sip, opened his ledger, flipped back to the front of the book, and continued. "Sal's knowledge of mason work was instrumental in a few of Franco's smash-and-grab jobs of the old banks and other lucrative businesses. Sal dealt only in the planning phase, and his brother Valentino had no idea. Sal and

I were making enough money to enjoy ourselves. There was dinner and dancing. We became regulars at the Las Vegas International Golf and Tennis Club when it opened in 1967. We even had our photos up on the wall in their clubhouse. It was beautiful and the golden age of Vegas. We saw Sinatra, Dean Martin, Elvis. The city was with gushing with headliners and entertainment. It was a blast.

In 1970, after almost ten years of solid earnings for the family, Sal had made enough to buy out a local bar, and I had made enough to buy out a restaurant, and we wanted out of the lifestyle. He and I went to our lieutenant above Franco and discussed our exit. We were given the OK by the Cleveland families after one last job, much to the disappointment of Franco."

I sat stunned at all this information. Gino went on. "But this time, Franco wanted a big score. He enlisted me, Sal, and two other fellas who worked as caddies at the Las Vegas International Golf and Tennis Club to take down a bank."

He took a large pull and finished his drink. "Sal explained how to break in through the old mortar. The two other guys with us went in first. Our information on the place wasn't good, and we came to find out the job wasn't sanctioned by the Cleveland families. The two guys who went in before me got shot by the guards and died. I was taken into jail for attempted robbery. Franco took off and wasn't implicated. I was sentenced to ten years and served three years. I hadn't said a word about the job to the cops and didn't spill on anyone."

He took a deep breath. "When I got out, Sal was waiting for me. Given this wasn't a sanctioned job, I was worried. Come to find out, Sal had squared everything with the family back in Cleveland. Sal had bought Sigaros. Franco tried to use Sigaros as a money laundering front after it was up and running. Sal called our old lieutenant to ask if the family had sanctioned the racket. Franco was operating outside of his directive, just like with the bank job. Being that he was still a top earner, he was moved back to Cleveland to be watched instead of... the alternative. Let's just say Franco was less than pleased to go back and made it well known he'd get back at Sal for it. But Sal had taken care of the bosses and lieutenants and wasn't to be touched. I have Sal to thank for my life and my new livelihood."

I took the first sip of my drink and asked, "What do you mean?"

"Had any one of the crew thought I was in with Franco, I would have been killed. Sal took care of it." With a little choke in his throat, he said, "He also leased the restaurant I was trying to buy before I went in and signed it over to me the day I got out. Sal's dad was Michael, but everyone called him Mickey. I named the place after him. I paid back every penny. I will always be in Sal's debt."

"Then why are you and Val not on speaking terms?"

Gino shrugged. "While he was in the seminary, Valentino got wind of what happened on the job and that two people died. He blamed me for keeping his brother in the business and putting Sal in danger." Gino waved his hands. "I hold no grudge with Valentino. I was the one who introduced his brother to the life. Sal knew the risk, and Valentino was just a kid still. I wasn't going to cause problems with Sal's family by confronting Valentino. Sal and I were straight ever since we got out and started our businesses in the early seventies."

I bowed my head. That was a lot to process. Sal and Gino were... mobsters. I knew Sal had a past and that he was a tough guy. But I never thought he was possibly connected with the mafia. Maybe the detective had a point.

I asked Gino, "What happened to the businesses you and Sal knocked over and the guys' families who died?"

Gino patted his ledger, pointed to the first page, and read it aloud. "'Payments monthly to widow Meryl Jackson, First Credit Union of Nevada, Las Vegas Sun, Fu's Laundry, and to the Golf Caddies Youth Program.' I pay this every month for the last forty years, and so did Sal. We couldn't find the second caddie's family to help them out, so we pay for a youth program. We never forgot or forgave ourselves for what we did back then. It wasn't right. The profit we made allowed us to run a business, and we've tried to give back ever since. We even sponsor the shops around us with no-interest loans and support the local new business owners with a forum to meet and network quarterly."

I nodded. "I need to figure out what happened when Sal left Sigaros the day he died. I need to see if Franco was the one who killed Sal. Do you know where I can find Franco?"

Gino looked me in the eye. "Listen, Leo, if you start down this road and if it is Franco that killed Sal, it's gonna be dangerous. Not a few scrapes or tussles. It could mean your life or those you care about. Franco is mean and holds a grudge."

I took his words seriously and returned his gaze. "Sal deserves to have his murderer found and arrested. It's the right thing. I have to do it."

Gino looked down and then back up at me. The place had started to clear out, and it was near midnight. I'd barely realized that we were the only ones at the back of the restaurant until Richie came over with the evening's receipts.

"I don't know what Sal was up to that day. The last I spoke with him was about canceling the poker game." He leaned in even though we were alone. "Be careful who you start to ask about Franco. When I called to let people know Sal was dead, I didn't hear anything from any of our old friends in or out of town that Franco was back. If he did come to town, he's been keeping it low-key. It's been more than thirty-five years since he's been in town." Gino leaned back in his seat. "There's a farmers market on Thursdays where some of the old crew may be able to give you some information. I'll let you know who to go to after some calls."

I leaned back and finished my drink. "Thanks, Gino. Wait. The farmers market?"

He nodded. "The mafia isn't gone from Vegas just because they don't run the casinos anymore, kid."

Surprised, I nodded. "Got it."

I got up to leave, and Gino was staring down at his receipts. I patted him on the shoulder and left.

I passed Richie on the way out. "Hey, Gino's been getting after his whiskey a little more tonight. Maybe splash a little more water in there if he asks for more."

Richie nodded. "I've been throwing in three ounces of water for each ounce of whiskey he's asked for in the last five hours."

I smiled. "Good man, Richie," and walked out of Mickey's.

23

It felt good to get up and move around again. My left leg was getting stiff from sitting there so long. I exited Mickey's and crossed over in front of Sigaros and saw a patrol car drive by in front of the plaza. I was headed to the street corner. *I wonder if Sal had a ledger like Gino. Maybe he would have put something in there about payments to somebody like Franco. Maybe that's what got him killed.*

I stuck my hand in my pocket and pulled out the spare key I neglected to give the detective. No one was around, and the patrol car had already gone by. This was my window to see if I could find anything in Sal's office that could give me a clue. I took a quick look around and headed toward the front doors of Sigaros. I lifted the police tape and cut through the official seal with my key, opened the doors, and went in. I figured if I was manager and going to be able to run the place, I should be able to enter whenever I felt like it. I walked in and pushed through the second set of double doors. I shined the light from my phone across the room. The place was still a mess, and I could still see the dried blood from where Sal was murdered. I stepped around and headed to Sal's office. If there was one place I was going to find a clue, it would be there.

I closed the door. The office was just as big of a mess as the front of the place. Looks like whoever tried to come at Sal never made it past his desk. The tables and chairs in his office were turned over, with the direction of the scuffle seeming as though it forced itself out into the main part of the lounge. I looked over the desk for any loose papers. There was nothing of importance. Opening the top drawers, it was the same. The safe was still open, and I briefly thumbed through the documents that were inside. It was all the same stuff I'd seen Sal put in there time and time again. There was no ledger. *I wonder if the detective took it.*

I turned from the safe behind the desk. I looked up at the row of books lining the ceiling shelf. I briefly shined my flashlight, but I couldn't tell if any had recently been moved or what types of books were even up there. I dropped my light to chest level, and it shined up on the mantle. *I wonder if he put something in that drawer when he came back.*

Walking over to the fireplace, I traced the frame of the mantle with my left hand around the corner to see if I could spring the drawer to open. It took three or four sweeps of my hand to finally find what seemed to be a lever that, with a small pull, popped open the drawer I'd seen Sal open. I looked inside with my light. There was nothing. *Where would you have put it?*

I started to feel uneasy. I didn't know how long I'd have before the patrol car returned. I closed up the hidden drawer, turned off my light, and carefully made my way to the front of the place. I poked my head slowly out from behind the double doors. There was no one there. I hurried out, locked the door, and quickly made my way to the end of the plaza, where I saw my cab waiting. I gave the man my address and headed home.

What was Sal up to that last day? Why was Franco back in town if not to seek revenge? I was too tired to think anymore. All I could do was hope to get to my bed and rest.

24

By the time my head hit the pillow, it was 3 a.m. The next sound I heard was a knock on my bedroom door.

Through the door, my mother asked, "Leo, are you gonna get up? It's after two in the afternoon. I know you were working late last night, but you can't let the whole day waste away."

I raised my head off the pillow and, with one open sleepy eye, I managed to get out, "I'm up, Ma. Thanks for waking me. I gotta go to church today by five, and then I'm going to try to hit Sigaros." My head crashed down on the pillow.

In a surprised voice, my mother said, "You're going to church?" There was a long pause. "Make sure to wear something nice when you go."

My voice was a little muffled as my head was still on my pillow. "I'm not exactly going to church, Ma. I'm meeting a priest. It's the brother of my boss. I'm meeting him for dinner."

With the same surprised tone, she said, "Oh well then... make sure you get a nice bottle of wine... but still dress nice."

Closing my eyes, I said, "You got it, Ma. Just five more minutes."

"Get your butt up NOW, Leo!"

I begrudgingly sat up and wiped the sleep out of my eyes, and replied, "Yes, Ma."

I staggered to my bathroom in my boxers and T-shirt. Looking at myself in the mirror, I could have used another twelve more hours of sleep. I peeled off the tape over my forehead and looked at the healing gash. It was clean and was probably going to heal nicely, hopefully without a scar. It still needed a bandage, but I left it off for now. I started to peel off the bandage over my left arm. It still looked raw. I think, had Val not put the antibiotic ointment, I would have been headed to urgent care. I decided to leave the tape around my ribs. I've had cracked ribs before, and those took ages to feel better.

I stepped into a lukewarm shower letting the cool water flow over me. I should have done this last night before I hit my bed, but I was too tired. Little pieces of gravel washed out of my hair, and I could see the blackness of the asphalt circling the drain. The water stung as it hit my open wounds but wasn't overtly painful. My thigh was bruised from my hip to almost my knee. It looked worse than it felt.

The shower was rejuvenating. I stepped out, redressed my bandages with a new set of topical antibiotics, and put on a pair of charcoal slacks and a white shirt with a matching sport coat. I dialed for a ride, given that my bicycle was out of commission. I was going to add it to the list of things that I needed to get to once this issue with Sal's murder was over.

I headed downstairs. I yelled out to whoever was still at the house that I was headed out.

My father walked by from his office on the first floor. "Headed to work?"

"No. I need to go see my boss's brother, a priest, over at a church near the Strip. Then I'll head into Sigaros to clean it up a little, I hope."

My dad bowed his head and looked at me. "I heard about your boss over the news. Sounds like it was pretty bad."

I didn't want to worry him or my mother. "Just one of those senseless random things, Dad."

"All the same, no job is worth your life. Just be careful." He headed out to the kitchen but turned and walked backward a few steps. "Your mother said to invite Sara over for dinner this Sunday. Make sure you ask her."

With protest, I said, "Come on, Dad. Leave it alone."

Turning to the kitchen and without looking at me, he said, "Fine. I'll let your mother know you didn't invite her."

With a sigh, I said, "I'll be home late. See you both later."

Before getting to the church, I stopped off and made sure I picked up a nice bottle of red wine.

I was a little early when I knocked on Val's door.

From behind the door, I heard Val yell out, "Just a minute." I distinctly heard the click of a phone hanging up before he answered the door.

"I'm sorry, I'm a little early. I hope I'm not interrupting."

Val was in slacks, a waist-high apron, a black button-down shirt without the priest collar, and a white kitchen towel slung over his right shoulder. "Not at all. I was just getting off the phone with the funeral parlor to plan for Sal's service this Friday. Come on in."

The aroma was overwhelming. Apparently, Val took his cooking seriously. The place looked like he had been prepping all morning.

I looked around his quarters and asked, "We did say five o'clock, didn't we? Am I late? You look like you've been working all day."

Val smiled and looked at me. "A good gravy takes all day." He waved me over to the kitchen. "Still lots of work to be done. Here take this." He threw an apron at me, and I caught it with my right hand and handed him the bottle of Merlot I brought with the left.

"Thank you, Leo. It should go well with our dinner. Go dice up the onions, carrots, and celery. The gravy is coming along nicely."

There was a large pot of boiled tomatoes, peeled and diced, that had been cooking on the stove. I could probably barely fit my arms around the pot. I turned to Val and asked, "Gravy? Isn't that sauce? Who else is coming to dinner?"

"Italians call sauce 'gravy,' son. I cook enough for at least the week and for any of our parishioners who are down on their luck and could do with a hot meal. Sal and I used to do this every Sunday when he came over after mass. We would chat about the week and any upcoming projects. Today, though, it's keeping my mind off the fact that I won't have those talks with Sal on Sunday anymore. I appreciate you coming over. How are your bumps and bruises doing?"

I walked over to the countertop, grabbed the cutting knife, and smiled back at Val. "Thanks to you, I'll heal up nicely. What would you say if we open that bottle of wine before dinner?

"Corkscrew's in the drawer to your right."

I found the corkscrew, opened the bottle leaving it to breathe, and set two glasses next to it, then made my way back to the cutting board with the vegetables. Val had gone back to checking on the pot on the stove.

After a few minutes, I poured the wine into both glasses and handed one to him. I raised the glass, "To Sal."

"To my brother."

We both sipped and savored the taste.

"Val, I by no means wish to be disrespectful, but I need to ask you a few things. Like I mentioned yesterday, I don't think Sal was killed in a robbery. I think he was killed out of revenge. I'm trying to find out who would have held a grudge against him and what happened during the day leading up to his murder. Do you by any chance know somebody named Franco Verga?"

Val looked at me for a good ten seconds and didn't lose my gaze. He walked back over to the bottle of wine and poured himself a full glass and took mine, and topped it off. "Leo, keep cutting the vegetables and hand them to me as you get them done." He turned back to stirring the pot, and I handed him the first round of vegetables that I cut. He didn't speak for another minute.

"Sal told me about Franco years ago, and I met him once when I came back to Vegas after the seminary. Sal was very specific in letting me know not to trust Franco if he ever came to ask anything of me. I think I need to start back when Sal and I first came to Vegas."

He took all the vegetables I'd cut, put them in a blender, added salt and pepper, and blended them up. He strained all the peeled and diced tomatoes from the pot and added them to the huge blender. Once it was mixed, he put it all back in a separate pot and set it to low after a boil. He poured himself another small amount of red wine. I hadn't touched mine after our initial taste, and my glass was still full. He motioned to the sofa, and I followed. He sat down in the armchair, and I took a seat on the sofa.

Val started. "Sal and I moved to Vegas with our father back in 1950. I was four, and Sal was almost seven. Our mother had died, and our dad couldn't find good work as a mason or contractor back in Chicago. But out in Vegas, he was able to get a well-paying job working as a mason at a new hotel going up, the Desert Inn. Given that Nevada had no state tax, a few extra bucks went further here than in Chicago. He was able to afford a caregiver for us while he worked, and we had a pretty good lifestyle. After the Desert Inn, our dad worked at the Desert Inn golf course and had a few other contractor jobs at the new hotels. I remember Sal and I walking through the new Dunes hotel when it opened, my dad pointing out all the different pieces he worked on."

Val paused and took a sip of his drink. "Dad died in 1960. Sal was just seventeen and dropped out of high school. He went to work at three different places just to keep us going. It was a miracle we weren't separated. He was able to pay the rent, feed, and clothe us, and even helped me graduate school. After high school, I helped him out on a few small jobs, and we were having fun."

Standing back up, he stirred the gravy and took a small taste, and walked back over.

Sitting back down, he continued. "It was our mother and father's dream for one of us to get into the priesthood, and Sal made sure to keep that hope alive. He got me settled into the seminary back east. It wasn't until later that I realized what he sacrificed and gotten himself into to keep us together. He was in debt with one of the mafia families from back east, from what I could figure out. He tried to keep me away from it all as best he could. When I was in the seminary, I'd gotten word that one of Sal's friends had been arrested, Gino. I called back home to ask, and I found out that a few people had died. I approached Sal, and he told me what he had been doing and about his friend Gino. Looking back, I was so full of anger at that time I blamed Gino, and sometimes still do, for Sal's misdeeds as a youth and the obligations that weighed on him later in life."

He took a sip of his wine before getting back up to check on the gravy. "Gino wasn't the one to blame. Sal made his choices. He lived with his consequences and tried to atone for any ill deeds. We sometimes spoke of them, and I gave him points of reflection. Leo, come help me with the pasta."

"Sure thing." I stood, taking my glass with me. "Did Sal say anything about Franco recently or any obligation he had the last time you spoke?"

Val put some meat into the gravy pot. "When I came back to Vegas as a priest, I only met Franco once. He approached me to try and stash some money at the church. I let Sal know, and he settled it with people back east, and Franco was sent away. Sal hadn't spoken about him for thirty-five years. Sal came to see me on Monday.

He said someone from back in the day had called him and that he needed to check on a few things. He had just come from updating some personal and business documents at his friend and lawyer John's office. Sal asked me to keep a book for him and that he needed to go to the farmers market coming up to talk to some people. He never mentioned Franco."

The aroma from the gravy was outstanding, and it was making my mouth water. Val grabbed some toasted bread that was sitting on the side and crumbled it into the pot as he stirred.

I swirled my glass around. "Sara got a call on Monday from a man with a raspy voice asking to speak to his good friend Sal. It was after that call that Sal left for the day and asked me to take over. I think it was this guy Franco. I think Franco had come back to town and confronted Sal, and that's how Sal got killed." Val kept stirring, and I continued. "When Sal left, he opened a drawer in his mantel and let me see him take a black leather notebook with a leather strap."

Val stopped and wiped his hands clean. He turned and walked over to his fireplace. "Our father taught us a lot about contractor work and how to lay brick and stone. Sal and I were pretty good. I helped him with his fireplace at Sigaros, and he helped me with mine."

On the opposite corner to Sal's mantel, Val touched the side of his own mantel, and a small drawer popped open. It was the same dimension as the other drawer. He lifted out a black leather-bound notebook with a leather strap.

He turned, holding the notebook gingerly in both hands, and faced me. "Sal told me to hold onto this. I've seen him with this book over the years, and he's always kept it to himself. I respected my brother's privacy. After he dropped off the book, I had assumed he was headed back to Sigaros." He looked at me with glassy eyes and reached out his hands. "Leo, if you can use any of the information in here to help get to the bottom of why Sal was killed, please... please help Sal. Promise me, though, that no matter where this leads you, you will do the right thing."

Setting my glass down, I crossed from the kitchen to the living room and placed one hand over the top of the book and one underneath, and gently took it away from Val. I looked down at the book and then to Val. "I promise."

Fighting back a choke, Val said, "Thank you." He looked back over to the kitchen and sprinted back. "Jesus, Mary, and Joseph! Leo! Get the big pot! This is about to burn."

25

The meal Val had made was delicious. The homemade pasta and sauce, rather the gravy, was amazing. I helped him prep about twenty extra meals. I know he had said that he had made enough for himself for the week, but he handed out every last portion to men, women, and children that came for evening mass. The light in his face when he gave the meals out was answer enough as to why he kept nothing for himself. Almost all the people there knew Sal, it seemed, and gave Val their condolences.

It was close to ten, and Val walked me out. I had the black leather book under one arm. It was quiet, and we spoke with soft voices so as not to feel overbearing in the empty church. Still, our voices echoed in the void of the space. He took my arm, escorting me to the door, and I could feel the weight of the last forty-eight hours wearing on him. He walked a little slower than this afternoon. If I'd have lost Gabe, I don't think I'd have been holding up as well.

With a bowed head, Val said, "Sal's service will be on Friday here at the church. I'd like for you, Gino, and everyone else at Sigaros to come. Would you please extend the invitation?"

Without hesitation, I said, "Absolutely."

"I would also like Gino to say a few words. If you don't mind, Leo, let him know that I'll be reaching out." Loss has a way of bringing people together, it seems. "If you feel comfortable, I'd like you to say a few words as well."

I was taken aback. "Thank you, Val, but I'm sure there have to be others that knew Sal for longer and better, for that matter, that would want to say a few words."

Nodding, Val continued. "There are, son." He was silent for a few more paces. "Sal told me the day he was killed that he planned for you to be manager and that if something happened, to give you the book."

I stopped and stood there a little wide-eyed. *So he knew something was coming.*

Val saw my look and grinned. He pulled my arm along. "I want you to speak—again if you feel comfortable—because you oversee Sigaros now, and you're trying to get to the bottom of what happened to my brother. In effect, you speak for Sal with your actions, and you will succeed him."

That thought weighed heavy on me as though a mantel had inevitably been placed upon me.

He stopped outside the church at the curb, letting go of my arm, and looked at me. "Just think about it."

I nodded. I looked down at the book. "Val, could you think of any other place that Sal would have kept any papers or information that could possibly tell me what else was going on before he died?"

Val looked out into the skyline and was quiet for a moment. The clouds reflected the glow of the neon across the city, and even at this time of night, it felt bright out. "Sal loved Sigaros. Besides helping others, the other enjoyment that he had was reading."

I was surprised to hear that. Sal never talked about any books or authors, well, at least to me.

"Sal used to say the books he read gave him perspective and taught him about how to live and act better in the world. Besides his bar and cigars, his books were his prized possessions." He smirked a little. "Our father used to keep our birth certificates and even kept spare cash in a book or two." Val squinted his eyes a little and turned to me. "I still keep my birth certificate in my bookshelf. I'd check Sal's collection."

"Thanks, Val. I'll check it out."

Val looked around. "Where's your bike?"

With a sigh, I said, "It survived, but it's in no condition to ride. I'll have to get it fixed before it's street worthy again."

Val stuck his hand in his pockets and took out a key ring with about ten different keys on it. He thumbed through and separated one from the group. "Here, take this. Sal wouldn't mind, and I won't be using it anytime soon."

I stuck out my hand, and he dropped a worn nickel key into it. I pulled it in closer, and it had the Lincoln star emblem on it. It was Sal's car.

I tripped over my next few words and thoughts. "I-I-I can't. That's Sal's. I'd feel wrong driving his car. I don't know…"

Val closed my hand over the open key. "As much as it pains me to say this out loud, it bears saying for the both of us. Sal's gone. Nothing will change this. Use what tools you can to get to the bottom of this. Sal would want that. I want that." His voice started to rise and become a little shaky. "It's not overstepping his things. He… has no more… things." He closed his eyes. "Sal is with our Lord and Savior. Use the car, Leo. Do what you need to bring him justice. Honor his memory, find his killer."

His hands were strong, and his knuckles were turning white as he spoke. I knew he was hurting, and he didn't mean to cling on so tightly. "All I ask is that you do the right thing. When you go out there to bring about justice for Sal, be careful. Don't get yourself into any trouble, and don't hurt anyone in the process." He paused. "Please, promise me." He realized as soon as he stopped talking how tightly he'd clung onto my hand and loosened his grip.

The words were of a brother, priest, and friend. They were full of pain, hope, and a plea for the world to make sense and be just.

I took the key and said the only thing I could, "I promise."

26

Sal's car was a two-door 1978 Lincoln Continental Mark V cream-colored with a beige interior. It was beautiful. I'd always admired his car. Now looking at it, I thought *Crap, this looks like what a mobster would drive. It must have taken a lot for Sal to get out of that life.*

Opening the door, the weight of the car was instantly noticeable. It was all metal. This was before fiberglass was placed in cars. This was more of a tank. I tossed the notebook onto the passenger seat. Sitting down was like stepping into a well-sat-in sofa. I didn't have to make too many adjustments, given Sal and I were relatively around a similar size. Well, maybe I needed to scoot a smidge forward. After getting my bearings, the size of the Lincoln set in. It was the size of a large SUV, and heading out of the church over those speed bumps that I now considered my nemesis, felt like small waves in a lake. This truly was like driving a boat.

My phone buzzed at me. I saw that I had two messages. I had one from Gino about twenty minutes ago, and the other one was from Sara just now. At the next red light, I looked down.

Gino's text read, "Go see Angelo tomorrow morning at seven at the farmers market in Summerlin. I told him to expect you."

Looking up at the light, it was still red. I know I shouldn't be texting and driving. I replied to Gino. "I'll be there. Spoke to Val. He'll be calling you. He'd like you to speak at Sal's funeral."

Sara had said, "I submitted the notarized papers to all the right offices, and the police should now have a copy. We can talk about opening Sigaros. Call me tomorrow, and we can discuss it and what Gino said. Remember, be careful!"

I sent a quick reply. "Got it. Call you tomorrow."

Well, if the police have all the right paperwork, it wouldn't hurt then to go back to Sigaros to check out Sal's bookshelf. I hit the gas as the light turned green, and the momentum of the car lurched forward. I'd have to get used to how heavy this was.

It was just like the previous night. I'd seen a patrol car drive by, and there was only one or two parked cars off to back of the plaza that looked empty. Still, I parked the car off one of the side streets and grabbed Sal's notebook. Walking up, I kept my head on a swivel for the patrol car.

The lights of Sigaros were all off, and I quickly opened the lock with the spare key and made my way into the main lounge keeping the light on my phone off until I had gotten this far. I closed the office door behind me, turned on the desk lamp, and put Sal's notebook down.

Sitting down at the office chair, I placed both hands on the side of the desk and took a deep breath. *I need to see if anything in here can give me any idea of what happened.*

I opened the black leather book. The first page had a similar look to Gino's book. The top right had the date Dec. 1, 1970. It had the same first entries: Payments monthly to widow Meryl Jackson, First Credit Union of Nevada, Las Vegas Sun, Fu's Laundry, and to the Golf Caddies Youth Program. Except in Sal's book, there was a circle in red around the youth program with a name written next to it, Roland Smith. The entry looked new and didn't match the rest of the ledger as I thumbed through. It was all written in the same neat unhurried handwriting. I'd seen Sal's handwriting when he was needing to jot something quickly, and this seemed the same. I kept looking through the rest of the ledger. Mostly it was names of other businesses. I recognized a few of them in the plaza and a few names from the customers who were regulars. I even saw a listing for a stall at a farmers market. Next to each one was an amount. Some had notations at the end saying "Paid in full" or "Forgiven." *Maybe Sal never got out of the life of a mobster. Was he a loan shark? Gino did say he and Sal would hand out loans and sponsor people.*

I looked up at the books on the shelf. I started to get up to grab the rolling ladder. A noise caught my attention before I could get out of my seat, and I stopped short midway between standing and squatting to see if it was just the chair. It was the sound of the front door slowly opening. I quickly turned off the desk light and cupped the flashlight over my phone to direct the light better and not let it bounce all over the room. Grabbing Sal's notebook, I made my way to the safest place I could think of to stash it, just in case. I found my way to the fireplace and ran my hand along the mantle, and with a push, I heard the noticeable click. Someone would have heard that too. I quickly placed the book in the drawer that popped out and gingerly closed it shut with the least amount of noise possible. Turning my phone's light off, I placed a hand on the office doorknob and turned it as quietly as possible.

I couldn't see anything or, more importantly, anyone. I stepped slowly and quietly out to the main lounge heading for the door. "Hey! You there! Stop!"

Before I could turn around or even fully raise my hands, I felt two stings in my right butt cheek. It didn't really hurt but was startling, given someone had just yelled for me to stop. It made me stand straight up. The next thing I noticed was a buzzing noise and a jolt. Not a little zap from an outlet or appliance. This was an excruciating electrical pain that made my right leg shoot straight out and all the other muscles in my body immediately tensed. I could feel every nerve in my body scream in unrelenting pain. I fell to the ground on my left side with a thud. The pain seemed to last forever. Finally, it stopped.

All I could do was lie on the ground catching my breath. It felt like I had just had the most intense work out of my life. The person standing over me was holding a Taser gun, and the wire leads were still attached to my backside.

In a panicked voice, I heard him say, "Don't you move! The police are right here." It was a pudgy middle-aged guy in a white button-down shirt, black tie, and trousers with what I could make out as a security emblem over his right chest. All I could do was nod and let out a breath. I didn't want this guy tasing me again.

Two officers walked in with their hands on their sides. The first younger officer asked, "What's going on here?"

The security guard, almost still yelling, said, "I caught this guy. I think he was trying to rob the place. I got him."

From the floor, with raised hands, I said, "My name is Leo. I work here. I'm the manager. I have every right to be here."

The security guard leaned in a little more with both hands on the Taser. "Sure, guy! That's what anyone would say who just got shot."

The police officers moved forward, each with one hand up. "Okay. Okay. Let's just put the Taser down."

Looking down at me, one said, "You say your name is Leo. Well, Leo, we didn't get any word the place could be opened. You'll have to come with us to the station."

Still on the ground, I nodded and gritted my teeth. "Take the Taser away from that guy, and you can take me wherever you'd like."

The officers stood me up. Every muscle ached, and my left arm and thigh were on fire. My right hamstring had a large knot in it. If I wasn't careful, a charley horse wasn't too far away. Rather than protesting, I thought it easier to go with the officers and let them cuff me and put me in the patrol car.

On the ride over to the station, I told the officers that Detective Thomas was the one who would know me. After radioing over, they brought me to an office with the title "Det. R. J. Thomas" written across the nameplate. With a knock, the officers walked in. "R. J., this guy says he knows you and that he's the manager of Sigaros."

Detective Thomas looked up from his desk. "Thanks, Tim. You can uncuff him. I got it."

Detective Thomas pointed at the seat in front of his desk and went back to finishing his paperwork. His office was bare except for a few pictures hung behind his desk: one from the police academy here in town, another with a detective's certificate, and the third was a certificate from the air force with a photo of him and his unit behind a sign saying "Wright-Patterson AFB Cleveland."

Without looking up and in a smug tone, he said, "So now you are the manager? I thought you said you didn't know Mr. Accardi had made you manager. Or were you lying to me?"

I rubbed my hands together, trying not to let my anger start to take over. My muscles were still screaming from the electrocution. I looked at the top of his head, as he still wasn't looking at me. "Sal did make me manager. I didn't know it until you told me yesterday. I signed the contract accepting the position. My friend Sara said she brought it over to the station today."

Still without looking up, he held up a paper next to the folder he had in front of him. "Got it right here. Sara, you say? She's pretty good. She knows her way around the legal department, it seems. You, as manager, do have a right to open the place as long as there are no stipulations in a will or other partners to claim the place, and it seems you have a spare key to the place." He finally looked up. "You don't know of any partners Mr. Accardi may have had, do you?"

I got the impression he was hinting at something. "No. Why? Has someone said they were his partner?"

"I don't have to share any information with you, Leo. On the other hand, you are obligated to tell me what you know about your boss and his current connection to any crimes if you want this mob hit to be solved."

I knew he wasn't thinking of anything else other than Sal being in the mob and attached to that lifestyle. Although the notebook in the office mantel showed he was lending money to various people and businesses, I still needed to figure out if that was true or not, and I needed to talk to the people he loaned money to.

I figured it was worth a shot to tell him about Franco. As calmly as I could I said, "I don't know anything about any connection to any crimes. What I do know is that a person named Franco Verga was in contact the day Sal died. Franco may have had something to do with his death." I paused, waiting for a reaction from the detective, but he just kept looking at me. "From what I can find out, Franco was an old associate of Sal's. I'd think looking to see if this person is here in town would be a good place to start."

This time the detective stood up with hands on his desk and leaned over, looking down at me. I would have stood to meet him, but my right butt still hurt.

"So you withheld information about your boss's recent activities and contacts."

"We get thirty messages a day at Sigaros. This was one of them. I looked into it, and I think it was this guy Franco."

Still standing, he asked, "Is this person's name attached with the message?"

"No, it was just listed as an old friend asking for 'my good friend Sal.'"

Detective Thomas sat back down. "That's a pretty weak connection to make to this guy Mr. Franco Verga. I need at least probable cause to even look into this person. Let me do the investigation." He went back to looking down at his paperwork. "With the paperwork that your friend Sara submitted and being that you are the manager, it looks like you can open Sigaros unless I find out something to the contrary. You can go." He waved a hand for me to go.

I got up. Rather I tried to stand. It was like I had just done a full week of squats. I thought it best to leave before I'd say something that got me into trouble.

I was at the door when Detective Thomas said, still without looking up, "Leo, keep your nose out of this. Your boss is dead and may have got what he deserved. Don't let his criminal life be the reason you lose yours."

My muscles were tensing up. The voice in my head was screaming to say, "No one deserves to be killed." I just gritted my teeth and shut the door, fighting back the desire to knock the detective out of his chair.

27

"What do you mean he's opening the place back up?"

In almost a growl, given the raspy nature of his voice, Franco annunciated each of the following words. "He who?"

"The manager of Sigaros. A guy named Leo. From what I just got told from our people, he's allowed to do so as the manager. Mr. Accardi named him in his ledger, and there's a notarized employment contract."

Franco patted down his already slicked back, mostly white and black hair. Seething from the news, he said, "I want Sigaros watched to see who goes back in before I get my hands on the place. If anyone goes in, make sure they come out hurting but not dead this time. Find out what you can on this manager of Sigaros. Follow him and report back to me. I'm sending you Michael and Sam. Vincente will take over when he gets to town."

"Understood, sir."

Franco sat in his chair, looking out the window with the phone in hand. Even at this distance off the Strip, it felt alive. He turned from the window, speaking to the two men in front of him. "Michael and Sam, I want you both to help Daniel. Follow Daniel's instructions. He'll know where to best place you for the jobs."

Without hesitation, the men said in unison, "Yes, boss," and turned to leave.

Franco turned back to the window. With the same raspy low growl, "Oh, and fellas, if you mess this up like you did when I asked you to bring my good friend Sal to me, I'll make sure it'll be the last. I can't believe you let that old man beat the hell out of all three of you."

The two men looked at each other and hurried out the door.

Franco picked up the phone. "Hey Vincente, thank you for the help with your guys. I'd like for you to come out here from L.A. tonight."

Vincente answered, "Still part of my debt repayment, I take it?"

"Yes, consider it paying off the vig. I need you out here to ensure I get what I came here for."

With a sigh on the other end of the line, Vincent said, "Sure thing. But if you want my help, you need to let me know what you're after.

With a pause, Franco said, "I have plans to run this town again. The mafia got soft back in the '60s and '70s and let corporations move in and take over all the profit. I'm not as soft as those old men. For my plan to work, I need Sigaros and, more importantly, the records that Sal kept. He's been the town's saint these last three decades handing out loans without interest and not even collecting if people couldn't pay. I've even gotten information he forgave loans asking those people to… oh, what's the way to say it? 'Pay it forward.' I intend to take over his books and collect payment in power and position."

Smirking, Vincente said, "Wow, this Sal seems like a real stand-up guy. I can see why you hate him so much."

With a quick response, Franco said, "I'm not asking for your opinion, Vincente! You owe me a debt. Payment is due without your comments, or I'll have no problem taking my payment in other ways. I don't think you'd like to see how your brothers would fair without my protection back home if you transfer the debt back to them." Now with that same growl, he said, "Is that understood?"

The phone was quiet for a moment. Vincente bit his lip. "Understood."

"Good. It is essential that we have our people stall the opening until I get a hold of the place. I've got something that will let me take it over and need twenty-four hours to put into play, and I want your help making that happen. If anyone gets in before I can get my hands on Sal's books, I've instructed those men you hired to make sure they get the point across that Sigaros is closed."

"I'm driving out now."

Franco hung up the phone and stood at the window looking out at the Vegas strip. "Soon, very soon."

28

Why, oh why, was this farmer's market so early in the morning? I swear morning comes so much faster when you have things that need figuring out. I could've slept for a week. My muscles still ached from being tased. Rolling over I stretched out my right leg. An immediate ball formed in my hamstring, and I could feel the muscles tighten up like a vice. I grabbed my leg out of reflex. My left arm let me know it still wasn't ready for so quick an action. Regardless, the charley horse outweighed anything else that mattered at this moment. I laid there holding my breath from the pain, working out the knot until it relented. Who said you need coffee to start the day?

Making it to the bathroom, I removed all the bandages and rib wrapping. Inspecting my right butt cheek, I had two spots of dried blood and a puncture site from the security guard's Taser. *Oh, I hope*

I meet that guy again. I'd love to shock the crap out of him. See how quick he is to tase people in the future.

The shower felt good. I just stood there in the hot water letting all my muscles take in the heat. My arm and forehead were healing up nicely. I placed a dry bandage over the left arm just in case the wound opened up. I was running out of nice dress shirts. The scrape on my head didn't need anything and was scabbing over. My right thigh had a nice purple look to it now, but the pain was negligible. I must have hyperextended my right knee when I got shocked, as it was a little sore with flexing.

I'd called Gabe when I got out of the police station to pick me up. I'd filled him in on why I'd gotten tased and for him not to tell our parents. I'd told him a little of what was going on, and he'd insisted on coming with me to the farmers market. Between being tased and exhaustion, I didn't have the energy to argue with him or to go back to Sigaros to pick up Sal's car.

Gabe was always an early riser. He was waiting outside the house by six thirty. I walked out the front door and down the few steps holding the side rail. It hurt more than I'd expected to walk downstairs.

Gabe looked at me concerningly. "You okay, Leo? You sure you want to do this today?"

I waved my hand at him brushing off the slow motion of my walk. "Just need to get moving a little. I'll be good."

I don't think he bought it. Shaking his head, Gabe said, "Okay, man. You don't look so great. Don't let Ma see you walking like that, or she'll be all over you with questions. Come on. I got you a coffee."

I was grateful for the ride and the coffee. I couldn't have gotten on my bike even if it was functional, and I needed a little more stretching if I was going to drive anywhere.

The market was across town, next to a park in Summerlin. We got there right at seven, and the place was already busy.

Gabe got out, and we stood at opposite sides of the car.

"So, who we seeing?"

"Gabe, thank you for coming. I don't want you involved more than you have to be. I'm going to meet a guy here alone. You can watch out for me and be here. But you won't be coming to this meeting. Is that clear?"

I guess my look was a little more serious than I expected because Gabe just raised his hands and, with an open palm, motioned to the entrance. "You know where this guy is going to be, at least?"

"I have a name and was just going to look at the information booth."

Luckily, Angelo's Produce was at the top of the list, and the little booklet had a directory of stall locations. Angelo's Produce was right in the far corner of the lot.

I made my way to Angelo's Produce, and it was packed. There were three rows of fresh produce. An older man was at the register, ringing people up. He had a little hunch to his shoulders with thinning white hair and was well put together in his button-down white shirt and slacks. I could see him and Sal hanging out. I approached the register and waited in the eight-person line. I saw the older man giving out orders to his helpers and greeting his customers like old friends. He gave out a few recommendations with each purchase of how best to cook a dish with it. I was about three people from the front of the line when the man saw me. He called back for one of his helpers to take over the register. I heard the young boy, who I assumed was his grandson, call back, "Sure thing, Nonno Angelo."

The man waved me over to behind the counter. "You must be Leo. Gino described you well."

I grinned. "Yes, you must be Angelo."

He smiled back. "If I must." He patted me on the shoulder, bringing me closer so others wouldn't hear. "I hear you wanted to ask me a few questions about Sal." He raised a finger, "Before I answer anything. Tell me why I should tell you anything about my friend Sal."

That's fair. I'd ask the same question if someone was asking around about a friend of mine that was killed.

I took a moment. "Sal was murdered. He was my friend. I think he was a good man. I want to see his killer brought to justice. No one deserves to be killed. The detective in charge of the investigation seems to have already made up his mind about Sal that he is or was a criminal. The detective doesn't seem to believe that people can change and that one's past doesn't dictate who they are trying to become, especially if that person is trying to do good." I paused again, thinking about all I had learned about Sal's life recently. "From what I've come to know of Sal's life, I do think people can change. I'm trying to make sure I'm right."

Angelo looked for a few seconds and winked. "Good. Ask your questions."

"First, I need to know was Sal involved in any loan sharking operations?"

Angelo smiled. "Sal? No. He was not a loan shark. Quite the opposite. Take a look around at the different vendors here."

I'd seen about thirty different vendors as I walked through to Angelo's Produce, and it was surrounded by a meat distributor, a homemade honey stall, fresh pastry shops, a Middle Eastern eatery, and a coffee roaster vendor. I'd noticed some of the names. Some of the vendors had shops that I'd seen around town.

"Between Sal and Gino, they helped these people start their businesses with loans when the bank turned their backs. Sal and Gino never charged interest and never came to collect. They even let some of the loans be forgiven without repayment. The only thing Sal or Gino ever asked was for those business people to pay it forward and help others start up. That's how this place has grown. That's how I got out of a previous life."

I turned back to Angelo. He was still looking around at the different stalls. I was glad to hear Sal and Gino had helped so many people. I asked Angelo, "Second, do you know if a man by the name of Franco Verga is back in town?"

Angelo kept staring at the different stalls.

"Angelo?"

Angelo turned back to me and came in a little closer. "I knew Franco Verga. I'd had run-ins with him back in the old days. He was a hard and vindictive man. Not one to cross. He was made to go back home after a job went south. Sal was instrumental in getting him out of town, and I know Franco blamed Sal for it. Vegas was a lot safer place without that guy. Sal and Gino getting out of the lifestyle along with the RICO act in 1970 paved the way for a lot of us here to get out of the Consa Nostra in Vegas. That included me. Sal gave me the loan to start up my own place, and now I have something more than stories of a misspent youth to give my grandson."

"We received a call at Sigaros the day Sal was killed from a man with a raspy voice asking for Sal. I think it was Franco. Do you know if Franco is back in town?"

"I know that his bosses back home just died and that there's a power struggle. The new bosses have yet to be established. The ones who died were the ones Sal took care of back in the day and were the ones keeping Franco out of Vegas and on a short leash. I have spoken to a few friends back there, letting them know Sal was dead. Those friends say they haven't seen Franco for the last week or so since the bosses died. If Franco isn't held back anymore, I'd say it's a possibility that he could be here."

That wasn't the answer I was looking for. "Thank you, Angelo. I appreciate it. I'll head back to Sigaros to see if I can find anything else that could tell me if Franco is back."

"I thought Sigaros was closed?"

"It is. But Sal named me as manager, and I'm opening the place back up. Thanks again."

Angelo grabbed my arm as I turned to leave. "Wait. Sal named you to take over?" He paused and gave me a more steadied look. "In our culture, the act of succession is a major deal. It's as much as when a boss names someone to take their place in the family. Do people know this, that you're running the place and opening it back up?"

I looked down at his hand, "Um, maybe. I let the police know last night when I was at the station."

He pulled me in closer. "Watch your back."

I was a little startled at the way he said it.

"You have a shadow, Leo."

I didn't turn around. I kept looking past Angelo. "If it's a guy that has glasses and short-cropped parted hair that looks a little like me but less awesome, don't worry, it's just my brother. He wanted to keep an eye out for me." I smiled, looking back down at him.

"No, that guy is watching your shadow. There's a guy in a black jumpsuit with white Adidas stripes that has the look of an enforcer. He is not a cop. Trust me, I used to send out the enforcers back in the day, and I know the look. I noticed him when you stepped into line."

His words gave me pause. Even though Angelo couldn't answer my question of whether Franco was back or not, given that I now had a tail, I was leaning a lot more strongly toward yes than when I first arrived at the market.

I patted Angelo on the arm. "I appreciate the heads-up. Sal's funeral will be tomorrow at St. Jude's Cathedral, by the way. Please come if you can."

Angelo replied, "Wouldn't miss it. Gino already called to let me know." He patted me on the face. "You have a little of Sal's bearings. Be careful, kid."

I headed back to the car, and Gabe met me on the way out. "You know someone was following you since we got here. You better be careful with whatever you're doing."

I was getting told a lot lately to be careful. I didn't want him to worry. "You're just imagining things. Come on, drop me off at Sigaros."

"Okay." I could tell he wasn't convinced. "Sure thing. We need to stop by the Las Vegas International Golf and Tennis club real fast. I have to pick up some plans."

29

The ride over to the Las Vegas International Golf and Tennis Club was fairly normal. Gabe and I talked about the different vendors from the farmers market, how crazy Mom and Dad were, and his work. He was excited about heading over to the club. He's been working on this project for the last year, and it was his big break in his architecture firm. He oversaw complete design with the renovation and expansion.

The club was well-established in town and been around since the fifties. Driving up to the gate, you could see a hidden image of the clubhouse. Past the guards' gate, you entered through a row of immaculately manicured hedges that led you to the clubhouse, and you were immediately transported back in time. Think 1960s design from when the Flamingo, Tangiers, and Sands were new casinos. It truly was a time capsule. As you approached the covered driveway, an attendant was already running out to get each door. The clubhouse had floor-to-ceiling gold-tinted windows caped with teak wood beams jutting out over the roof with columns of white limestone in between each section of the building.

An attendant opening Gabe's door said, "Good morning, sir. We weren't expecting you today."

Gabe replied, "Good to see you, Jeff. Just picking up some plans for the office."

The young man nodded and took Gabe's keys. "I'll leave it up front."

The attendant that opened my door was younger than the boy who took my brother's keys. I nodded. Fixing my ponytail, I turned to my brother, "You make them call you sir? You're a dick."

"Shut up. I've told them to call me Gabe, but they refuse, and anytime someone calls me by my last name, I feel like they're asking for Dad.

Squinching my nose, I replied, "Yeah, I feel the same."

Walking into the foyer, you were greeted with the perfume of roses that were at the center of a large round oaken table. The room was the tallest part of the building and was open and grand and at least two stories tall. It was flanked by green velvet floor-to-ceiling drapes and had a beige marble floor. There were four separate areas for seating with deep leather armchairs. I noticed, too, that there were security cameras mounted just like in the casinos. They were unobtrusive but placed well enough where the entire layout could be seen.

"I'll be five minutes. Come inside and check out the place if you'd like."

Gabe walked me over to the clubhouse bar. It was the same oaken color and in a U shape, with one side open to the golf course through the gold-tinted windows and the other side against a wall lined with photos of members and celebrities throughout the years. I took a seat a few chairs down from Gabe, looking at the wall as he asked if he could talk with Jeffery.

Sigaros could do with an upgrade and maybe even an expansion. It needs cameras. If there'd been cameras rolling the night Sal had been killed, I wouldn't be all over town trying to figure this out.

My phone rang, and I looked down. I hadn't recognized the number, but it was a local call, and I answered. The voice at the other end sounded like Sal's for a moment, "Leo, this is Val."

"Val. Hey, everything good?"

"Everything's good, thank you, Leo. I wanted to ask if you'd thought about speaking at Val's funeral tomorrow. It'll be at four tomorrow, followed by a little get-together at the church."

I paused. I'd been avoiding thinking about talking at the funeral. I didn't like funerals. The ones I'd gone to as a kid when my grandparents passed were so heavy, and I'd seen the strain it put on my parents. "I don't know, Val. You sure you want me to?"

"I do, Leo, and… I think Sal would too. Please. I'd appreciate if you did."

Val had said it with such hope and plea that I didn't have the heart to decline. "Sure thing, Val. It'd be an honor."

With an audible change in his tone, Val said, "Good. Tomorrow at four I'll see you at the church. You'll talk after Gino and the last reading."

"I'll be there."

"Thanks, son."

That reminded me I needed to let Kate, Mia, Mike, and Sara know. Still on my phone, I pulled up my texts. I was walking around the end of the bar. I found myself reading a plaque labeled "History of the Club." There were photos of Bing Crosby, Dean Martin, Sinatra, Bob Hope, and other old celebrities in their prime playing at the club.

I sent out a group text letting them know the timing of the funeral and where to go.

Looking up, I'd seen a petite balding man approaching Gabe. He was likely middle-aged with a starched white shirt, a blue blazer, and a handkerchief that matched his shirt. "Hello, Gabe. I didn't expect you."

I paid little attention to the start of the conversation. My phone buzzed, and I looked down. It was Sara calling.

"So we need to talk about tomorrow. You need to get all the supplies to clean up for Sigaros. I have everything ready that I can think of legally for us to move forward with the opening. But if we can locate Sal's will to have documentation that Sigaros can be kept running postmortem as a corporation, then you can continue to act on its behalf."

I swear she barely breathed between sentences and kept on going. "I bet if we clean up the place before and after Sal's funeral, we can open on Saturday. I'd like to do a little memorial for him that day."

The pressured speech was a little much. I decided to defuse her a little. "Well, it's nice to hear from you too. I'm well. How are you?"

Dripping with disdain, Sara said, "Leo, we've got things to do. Yes, I hope you are well. Gino filled me in on the plans for the funeral. I already messaged everyone." With a questioning tone, she said, "He also said you were checking a few things out at a farmers market today. You'll have to tell me later. Anyways, I've got to run. I'm finishing up some work for my class tonight and have to run out later to get a dress for the funeral."

I'd never seen her in a dress before. "So... a dress?"

"Yes, a dress. Keep your mind out of the gutter, Leo."

I grinned. "Fine. Fine."

"Be at Sigaros to help clean up at 10 a.m. Make sure you have cleaning supplies for everyone; mops, rags, disinfectant, Windex, you know... everything."

"So... who's the manager?"

With a sigh, she answered, "Leo, just make sure you get all the stuff," then hung up.

Walking back to where Gabe was talking with, who I assumed was the manager of the club, I noticed a picture on the wall. It looked like all the rest. A group of guys in golfing gear standing in front of one of the club's many picturesque greens with golf caddies in the background. Except this one had the names Franco Verga, Luigino Rossi, and Salvatore Accardi, along with the caddies Roland Smith and James Jackson. I stopped. They were all here. I'd remembered now that Sal used to work here and, from the looks of it, played here as well. Those must have been the two caddies who got killed on the robbery. I'd recognized the name Jackson from Gino's ledger of payments to a widow Meryl Jackson. The other name, Roland, was from Sal's ledger that was circled in red. I took out my phone and snapped a photo of the picture. Sal and Gino looked so much younger. I made sure to pay attention to the image of Franco. He was medium height, lean, and his slicked back hair made him seem greasy even just from the black-and-white photo.

Gabe spoke to me from a few feet away while I was still taking the photo. "I'll be back. Just headed to the office."

I waved him off, and the man who was speaking to him walked over, and it was just him and me in the bar.

"So, you're Gabe's brother. He speaks a lot about you. I'm Jeffery. I manage the club."

"Nice to meet you. Leo's the name." I stuck out my hand, and he shook it firmly.

He placed a hand on my right shoulder and left it there. "I see you noticed some of our past members here on the wall. We just put this one up last week. Mr. Accardi was a big supporter of our caddies youth program, as is Mr. Rossi. We recently found a roster of all our caddies going back to 1960 in our financial department and were able to put their names up with the photos of the members. In a somber tone, Jeffery said, "Mr. Accardi will be missed."

I asked, "This other man in the picture here... Mr. Verga. By any chance, he hasn't been around here lately?"

His hand made its way down to my lower arm, and he turned to look at me. "What a coincidence. A representative of Mr. Verga called just this morning to reinstate his membership. He was inquiring about the recent renovation and the architect working on the place. He asked if Gabe had shown up here today."

The hair on the back of my neck started to stand up, and I could feel goosebumps form over my arms. *Franco is back!* A little sense of dread set in as my thoughts started to flow. *He's asking about Gabe. If Franco was asking around about Gabe, he was likely asking around about my parents and everyone else I was close with, especially from Sigaros.*

I tried not to let my sense of panic show. "Did this representative give their name?"

"He was very pleasant. His name was Vincente, I believe."

"Thank you, Jeffery."

Jeffery let his hand slip down to mine, and he pulled himself in closer. "Gabe mentioned you are the new manager of Sigaros. I'm so sorry for your loss." He placed his left hand over my chest. "Grief after the passing of a figure such as Mr. Accardi can be difficult. It's important to have support and an outlet to let loose one's emotions at times like this." He stepped in a little closer.

A little light bulb went off in my head. Now I've been hit on by guys before. Not gonna lie; I do attract an occasional few with my ponytail and reddish beard. I find it flattering but it's not my wheelhouse. I was not expecting this from Jeffery given the way he was around Gabe.

As politely as I could, I took his hand off my chest and said, "Jeffery, thank you so much for your concern. I appreciate it. It is a lot to process. Gabe and I are on our way to plan for the funeral and get Sigaro's up and running again."

I saw Gabe walking over from the office. "Oh, look. Here he comes now."

Jeffery abruptly removed his hand from mine. He turned to greet Gabe and was a little flustered. "Found the plans, I see?"

Gabe replied, "Yes, thank you. Leo, all ready?"

I snuck past behind Jeffery and slapped him on the shoulder. "Nice to meet you."

Gabe and I headed to the door when Gabe turned and said, "Oh, Jeffery, please tell your wife and kids we'll be here next week for the club's family night. My wife and kids had a blast last time with the family."

Jeffery smiled and waved. "Looking forward to it. Bring Leo along if you can."

30

ack in the car, I turned to Gabe. "So, your buddy there is a friendly guy."

"Yeah, he's always inviting us to the club for family nights or other events. He's social at the club, but then I guess he has to be given he's the director."

"You've never caught any strange vibes from him? Maybe, some innuendos or a lingering hand per se?"

With a furrowed brow, Gabe said, "No."

"Well, just be aware of your surroundings when you're around 'social Jeffery.'"

"Okay, you're being weird. Well, weirder than normal."

"Just pay attention if he asks to speak with you alone. Could you drop me off at Sigaros? I have to pick up my car. I need to run a few errands. I need to get supplies to clean up Sigaros tomorrow. Also, I was thinking of going to the security store and picking up some cameras and some alarm equipment, and I need to go home and work on the eulogy for Sal for tomorrow."

"Busy day, brother. I'm real proud of you stepping up to the plate, by the way. You really seem to want this. I'm happy for you. I haven't seen you this motivated before."

I paused and took that in. He had a point. Had the going gotten tough like at the other ventures I had tried, I would have stopped halfway through. I hadn't even looked at my own little idea book over the last three days. It didn't seem to matter right now. What mattered was getting to the bottom of proving Franco murdered Sal for his books and trying to prove it to the detective to clear up Sal's murder.

"Thanks, Gabe. I appreciate it."

"Wait. You have a car now?"

"Well, a car of sorts. I'm borrowing Sal's old Lincoln Continental Mark V. His brother said it was okay."

Gabe nodded. "Nice. Well, if I ever die, you can let people borrow my car if they'd like. It's not much, but it's reliable."

I thought about that for a moment. With everything going on and knowing that Franco was starting to ask questions about people I cared about, I don't know what I would do if any one of them got hurt. Sal was dead and, that was enough. I needed to clean this business up and quickly.

Gabe said, "Hey, if you want to look at some cameras, I have a guy that I used for the club, and I'm sure he'd be more than happy to help with any security equipment. He even has some amazing audio devices that he can place in power outlets."

I gave Gabe a raised eyebrow. "A power outlet recording device? Come on."

He raised his right hand as if swearing in at a courtroom. "I'm serious. In the power outlet. Give him my name and let him know you're my brother, and he'll take care of you. I'll send you the address to his store and the number."

"Thanks, Gabe, I appreciate that."

If I am truly going to run and manage Sigaros, I need to think beyond solving Sal's murder. I need to think of keeping what he had alive and growing it. Without growth, things tend to fade away. Vegas is ever-changing, and Sigaros needed to change with it.

"Hey, Gabe, when you have some time, and maybe after the funeral, I'd like to talk to you about seeing if we could expand Sigaros. I'd like to get your thoughts."

Gabe did a double take as he was driving, "Wait. Did you just offer me a job? Wow. How the tables have turned." He smiled with that big stupid grin.

"Shut up, you. I'm not saying you'll get the job. I need to get a few bids first."

"Gee, with your own family, you play hardball."

I smiled back. "I have to look out for Sigaros."

Gabe dropped me off. I followed up on the supplies Sara asked me to get and went to Gabe's security store guy. He gave a good deal on security cameras with built-in links to alarms. By the time I was done, it was already nine o'clock. Luckily, Ma had leftovers, and I ravaged the kitchen. Tomorrow was going to be a long day, too, and thinking on how famished I was today, I decided to call in an order for food for everyone tomorrow at Sigaros.

Now for the hard part of the day. Trying to think about how to write Sal's eulogy.

31

I guess when you have obligations that need taking care of, your body knows when it's time to get started. I was up before my alarm. Now I haven't set an alarm in years. I did last night, knowing how busy today was going to be with cleaning up Sigaros and the funeral.

Even though I was up, my body was still tired. Writing Sal's eulogy took me the better part of the evening and into the early morning. My muscles still ached from being tased and the fall from the bike. It still hurt to take a deep breath but not as much as yesterday.

The shower was rejuvenating. I cleaned up and wore a T-shirt and jeans and packed my suit for later for Sal's funeral, and headed out to Sigaros.

As I opened the front door, my mother poked her head around from the kitchen. "Leo? You going to work already?"

"Yeah, Ma, busy day with getting Sigaros back in shape, and I have my boss's funeral today, and I'm giving the eulogy. I'll be back late."

"Well, have as good of a day as you can, Leo. I'm sorry about your boss."

"Thanks, Ma."

I turned to leave when she yelled out. "If you haven't done so already, invite Sara to dinner tomorrow."

Crap. I completely forgot. It was no use arguing. "Sure thing, Ma."

On the ride over to Sigaros, all I could think about was the speech I was having to give, and went over as much as I could recall without getting it out of my pocket. *Should I talk more about his past, or maybe not? Should I talk about how he started out or his friends?* I must've revised what I was going to say ten times in my head.

Mike, Kate, Mia, Sara, and Gino were all waiting out front when I pulled up to Sigaros in Sal's Lincoln.

Gino smiled. "Not many people can pull off driving up in that old thing besides Sal and I, but it looks like it fits you well. Where was it?"

I smiled back, getting out of the car with the packages of security system supplies in two large bags. "At the church. Val is letting me borrow it for a little. Hey, Gino, you order a security guy to watch the plaza?"

"Yeah, why?"

"He's a little trigger-happy with his Taser and needs a little training."

Gino saw my limp as I got out of the car and bit his lower lip, smiling.

Straightening up, I turned to everyone. "Listen, thanks everyone for coming today. It's a bittersweet day. Sal's gone, and we'll be saying goodbye to him and will continue to do so even after today, in our own way. What we won't be saying goodbye to is what Sal stood for; Sigaros and the people he helped. That includes all of us. Let's get the place back up to Sal's standards and have it ready for tomorrow."

They all nodded without saying a word. Tearing away the new police tape and cutting through the security paper between the doors, I unlocked Sigaros and opened both doors wide. Holding the door, I let them all walk in before me.

Gino was last and turned to me before going in. "Nicely done, Leo, but they'll need you even more when they get inside."

I nodded back to Gino. I looked around before I walked in to make sure there wasn't a Taser-eager security guard behind me. They had all stopped at the foyer and were looking over the place.

After giving them all a minute, I spoke up. "Mia and Kate, clean and straighten up the tables and chairs. Mike, open all the windows and doors and let the light in, and once you're done, get the cleaning supplies from Sal's car for Mia and Kate, and then you can start cleaning the floor. Sara, you're in charge of getting the bar back in order. Also, Sara, I'll need a copy of the paperwork you submitted showing me as manager in case anyone comes to inquire. Gino, you're with me. We'll be in Sal's office cleaning up. Grab one of these bags." I looked at each one of them. "Remember, we're going to open tomorrow. Ask each other and me for help if you need it."

Sara broke the silence. "Pay up, everyone. He got here before eight. Mia, you owe me an extra ten."

I guess I shouldn't have been surprised. I'd have bet against me, too, up until a few days ago. Still, I had to know. "Why does Mia owe an extra ten?"

"She bet you'd also forget the cleaning supplies."

I turned to the rest of them. Mia's head was down.

"Mia!"

In a meek voice, she said, "Well, when Sal asked you to get it before you'd forgotten."

I replied, "Well, that's true... Okay, it should've been a safe bet."

With a grin, Sara leaned in close and said to me, "I told her the difference was this time I was the one who told you to get the supplies."

I just shook my head at her. "All right, everyone, get to work. I've got food coming for everyone at noon, and we're stopping at three to get ready for the funeral."

Mike looked up. "Food? Wow, thanks, Leo. Promise, won't bet against you again."

I patted his back on my way to the office. "See that you don't."

Gino got there before me. I walked past him to the desk and noticed him looking out across the room. He wasn't as much looking at anything but rather deeper in thought.

"You know, Leo. I had my first meal after getting out of jail with Sal here at the poker table. I laughed so hard when he told me how he'd gotten Franco to leave town." Turning to the rest of the room, he pointed behind him, "He gave me the papers to the restaurant at that couch." He cleared his throat. "Great times. Such great times I had here with Sal."

I stopped unpacking the bag and looked over at him. "Me, too, Gino."

He paused for a little longer, letting the memories of those moments linger, then cleared his throat again. "What's in these bags?"

"Security update for Sigaros. I'd been talking to Sal since I started here about upgrading the security, and my brother gave me a line on someone who gave me a deal on an alarm system with some fun little gadgets that I intend to get up and running now. You're helping me with it. I know where I'd want cameras and alarm access, but I want to hear where else you'd want them if you were running the place. Once that's done, we'll clean up the office."

Gino looked down at the bag with an approving nod. "I've got a few thoughts."

We all got to work. The place was coming together nicely. Mia, Kate, and Mike had gotten the place looking great. Sara had restocked the bar and called all the main distributors to start coming in next week. Gino was handy and pretty computer-savvy. He helped me set up the online process for the alarm system, and I'd gotten most sensors and cameras up and running.

Sara came walking into the office. Even with working all morning long, she didn't look like she had even broken a sweat and still smelled of jasmine. "Hey, Leo, here's the papers you asked for regarding verification of the manager's position. I think we still need to find better documentation from Sal's will to make sure we can keep the place open. Here is the list of the distributors coming next week, the supplies we're low on for the bar and cigars—Tony sends his condolences, by the way—and here's the money pouch from the day..." she paused, and I caught her turning her face away for a moment, "... from Monday."

"Hey, Sara. You okay? Why don't you sit down for a minute."

Gino looked over. "I've got to run to the restaurant. I'll be back in twenty." Gino always could read a room.

Sara waved off the invitation to sit. She looked back at me with glassy eyes. Her voice had a little shakiness to it with a hint of anger. "Why'd this happen, Leo? Who the hell would want to kill Sal?" She threw her hands up, letting them land helplessly on her thighs. "And for what goddamn reason?" She leaned on the back edge of the couch.

I paused, looking at her. *If I tell her about what I've found out, she'd want to help. If I didn't tell her and she found out some other way, she'd try to look into it herself anyways and be pissed I didn't tell her.*

"I-I think Sal was killed over a book he kept. A ledger of loans he gave out." Sara looked at me a little surprised. "He's been helping people out over the years with getting their businesses up and running or giving personal loans." I raised my hand up to stop her before she could speak. "He wasn't charging interest. He even let some of the loans go without having to be repaid. He wasn't into anything illegal."

In a rushed voice, she asked, "Who in the hell would want the book or ledger or whatever?"

I raised both my hands up. "Again... I think there is a guy who Sal and Gino used to work with that came back to town who wants the book. The guy with the raspy voice that called. He probably wants it to start collecting on the loans and to use Sigaros as a starting off point. Someone named Franco Verga. I think he's the one who killed Sal."

She sat there, her eyes focused on the ground. "I know Sal helped people out. Hell, he helped me with my school loans." She looked up at me. "You really think this guy wants to use that stuff to shake people down?" She stood and said, "We can't let Franco get the book or Sigaros. Do you know where to look for the book or the will?"

I looked at her for a moment debating whether or not to tell her the truth. "I have a pretty good idea where the book is, but I can't get a lead on the will."

She started to head to the safe. I stopped her, holding her arm with my hand. "I've checked the safe, but there's nothing there."

Looking up to the books lining the ceiling, I said, "But when I was talking with Val, he said Sal's other prized possessions were these books. I just finished checking the ones on the back wall above the desk and was going to look above the mantel."

"Sal told me before how much he loved some of these books." She smiled and said, "I'll grab the ladder."

I was halfway up when Gino knocked, saying the food had arrived and asked Sara to help. She motioned for me to stay to see what I could find while she helped Gino.

Just like the shelf on the back wall, above the shelf there were dust-covered volumes of classics. Some I've thumbed through in school, others I'd never heard of. Sal had books above the back wall that read like a library of great reads that changed the world; *Epic of Gilgamesh*, *Odyssey*, *The Art of War*, even the Bible, the Quran, and the Bhagavad Gita. On the wall above the fireplace, the books looked to be just as classic. The first three were all dust-covered; *A Vindication of the Rights of Woman*, *The Autobiography of Benjamin Franklin*, and Marcus Aurelius' *Meditations*. I thought to myself, *Man, these are heavy reads. I could see why Val said they gave him pause for reflection.*

But the fourth and sixth ones had been moved in the last few days, given how the dust was shifted on the shelf. I grabbed for the first one titled, *Confessions* by Saint Augustine. I immediately opened it and scanned through it like a flip-book. Halfway through, there was a folded paper. It was the same red ink in the beginning of Sal's ledger, and the paper looked like it was the same dimension and coloration as his book.

Roland Smith: 24 years old. Widowed. Son: Roland Junior aged 5 at time of death. Last address: North Las Vegas Foster Care. 281 Ann Road, North Las Vegas 89030.

I snapped a photo of it with my phone. *He'd found the name of the other caddie that was killed. He had a son. I bet you Sal was looking to find the kid. He was probably trying to set things right.* I flipped through the rest of the book. Nothing.

I reached for the other book that had been disturbed. It was Thomas Paine's *Common Sense. Now this one I've read.*

Just as I was about to grab it, Mike walked in quickly. "Leo, you'd better get out here."

"Mike, one minute. I'm not hungry."

"No! Leo. We need you out here now." Mike hasn't ever raised his voice that I can remember.

I stopped, then hurried down the steps and out to the main room.

Kate, Mia, and Sara were behind the bar looking at the entry doors. Five feet in front of the bar was Gino standing in defiance, facing three men who had entered. One of the men was Detective Thomas, one I'd seen at the farmers market, and the other was an older man whose younger picture I'd seen on the wall at the golf and tennis club. It was Franco.

I came around to Gino's side. He had his shoulders pulled back with hands clenched at his side and was locking eyes with Franco. Franco was smiling smugly back. Apparently, I'd missed introductions and any part of the conversation that had made Gino angry.

I decided, *What the hell, might as well jump right into it.* With a smile and a hand on Gino's shoulder, I said, "Well, Detective Thomas, nice to see you. I see you brought Mr. Franco Verga and his friend to help clean up. That's so good of you." I looked at the beefy man in the track suit standing next to Franco and pointed at him. "You I saw yesterday. How'd you like the farmers market? You wouldn't be Vincente, would you?"

Franco dropped the smug smile for a moment and turned his head ever so slightly toward the man on his right. The beefy man didn't move or say a word. Franco's picture didn't do him justice. He was still as slim and greasy looking as his picture on the wall, and time had only changed his color of his hair and made some of his facial features more pronounced. But it was his eyes that captured the essence of who he was. They were a piercing blue that seemed to stare straight through you with a hunger behind them as if he wanted to take everything.

In a raspy well-controlled voice, Franco spoke. "No, Leo. I'm not here to clean up." He looked behind me at Sara, Kate, and Mia. "But I do appreciate you straightening up my place. My good friend Sal would have appreciated it."

Detective Thomas, holding a handful of papers, spoke up, looking directly at Gino. "As I was just about to explain to Mr. Rossi before he told us to leave, Mr. Verga here has just provided a legal document verifying him as a partner in Sigaros. Being that he is the remaining owner, he has the right to do what he wishes with Sigaros."

I stood there stunned at the words. Without raising my voice, I asked, "May I take a look at the papers."

He handed them over without hesitation. I thumbed through the document.

I yelled back to the bar. "Sara, can you come here and look at these and give me an idea if this is a legal document and has bearing."

Sara crossed over from behind the bar. I could hear her boots approaching from behind and looked up to see both Franco and what could only be his enforcer watch her like a predator.

Looking through the papers, she said, "Yeah, looks like this was submitted just yesterday, and the proof of partnership was listed from an agreement from 1970."

Gino crossed over to Sara and looked at the documents.

Sara looked up at Franco. "I'd like to look at that original agreement."

With gritted teeth, Gino spoke up, looking directly at Franco. "That agreement wasn't for Sigaros. It was for the arrangement on the bank."

With hands held behind him, Franco stepped forward, looking directly at Sara, "Gladly. You'll see all the documentation is in order. They're down at the county office being placed as official records. You or whoever else can view them on Monday. But until that time..." Franco walked up and took the papers out of Sara's hands, "I'd like for all of you to leave my place now." Walking away and with almost a sneer, he said, "I've things to do."

He just stood there smiling at her.

Sara shifted her weight into a boxer's stance, and I saw the beefy man, who seemed to have a few recent bruises on his face, start to move. I stepped in between Franco and Sara.

Franco raised a hand, halting the approaching enforcer. "It's okay, Daniel."

I spoke up and, in as calming a voice as I could, said, "All right, everyone, grab your stuff. We'll leave and work on looking into how to get Sigaros back on Monday. We should get ready for Sal's funeral." I looked straight at Franco with my last sentence. "Sal would have wanted us to handle this honorably."

Everyone grabbed their stuff and headed out the front doors. Gino and Sara glared at Franco as they left.

As I was leaving, Detective Thomas stopped me, saying, "Leave your spare key here with Mr. Verga."

I stopped and placed my key on the table. I turned to see Franco heading to the office and said to Detective Thomas, "Anything yet on who killed Sal?"

"Nothing yet. We're still looking into the activities of Mr. Accardi or criminal activity in the area."

"Well, I'd start with the office if I were you."

I turned and left.

32

Outside Sigaros, we all stood huddled around each other. The conversations ranged between outrage, sorrow, panic, and disbelief. I agreed with each one of the conversations, but this wasn't the time for any of it.

In a soft voice, I started to speak. "We will all work together to get Sigaros back. This is a bump in that road. Right now, it's time to go pay respects to a good man. Let's all get ready for the funeral." Sometimes, speaking in a softer voice carries the greatest weight, and it silenced everyone.

Gino patted me on the arm, and Mike, Kate, and Mia started out. Sara was standing next to me, arms folded, tapping one foot on the ground. I placed a hand on her shoulder. She shrugged it off. "How could you just stand there, Leo? That was the guy. That was the guy that killed Sal. We can't just let him take the place."

"Sara, you're the one who told me to be careful. The smart thing to do is to verify the document, and if it's not legal, we can get the place back. The way Gino made it sound was that those documents were likely from a different arrangement, and Franco is likely lying to try and get his hands on Sal's ledger."

Sara looked down at the ground and unfolded her arms. "No, you're right. Damn it."

I looked at her. "Plus, when we do get back in there, we can follow up on the books. There were two books on the shelf above the mantle that were moved. I only had a chance to look at one of them. It had a name of someone Sal was looking for from a long time ago."

Her eyes lit up. "Give me the name and information. Maybe I can run it through some of my legal resources."

I sent her the photo and said, "I'm hoping we can get a look at the other book before Franco searches the place."

Sara looked back over at Sigaros and said, "Come on, let's get going to the funeral."

I had just enough time to go home, shower, and change. My left arm and leg were healing up nicely, and I only had a sharp pain over my ribs with too deep a breath. My right butt still hurt, though. I arrived with fifteen minutes to spare. On my way in, I recognized one of the Monday night poker game regulars. It was John: Sal's friend and lawyer.

Running to catch up with him, I tapped him on the shoulder. "John, sorry. Can I bother you for a minute before the service?"

John was average height and build, balding, and about Sal's age. Turning to me, he said, "Leo, sure. What's up?"

"I'm sorry to do this right before the funeral, but I need to ask. Did you see Sal on Monday?"

He nodded. "Yeah, he came to the office to update some of the paperwork related to Sigaros. He also made changes to his will. We made the changes, and he took it with him when he left, saying he'd give it to me later at the poker game, but then he canceled, saying he'd give it to me next time he'd see me." He bowed his head. "I never thought that'd be the last conversation I'd have with him."

"I'm sorry, John. It's been a rough few days for all of us with Sal gone. Did he say what changes he was making? Did he say anything about a partner Franco Verga?"

Shaking his head, he said, "No. Sal had no partner listed in any paperwork. He only changed information pertaining to the role of the manager in the event of his passing in the business agreement for Sigaros, and in the will, he made some changes to his personal effects. I'm not legally allowed to say anything until the new documents and will are presented and read."

"Thanks, John, I appreciate it. I'll see you inside." I turned to head inside.

John grabbed my arm before I left. "Val told me you were talking at the funeral. I'm glad. Sal would have liked that. He was very fond of you, Leo. I think he saw a lot of himself in you and the potential." He let my arm go and simply said, "Thanks."

I nodded back to him, trying to fight back the lump in my throat that was forming.

Walking inside, I was greeted by Val. In such a public setting, I thought it best to refer to him with his proper title. "Father Accardi, my condolences."

He smiled back at me, grabbing both my hands. "Thank you, Leo. You have a spot up front for your part. I'll see you up there."

On my way up, I heard my name called and looked down the pew but couldn't tell who yelled out. I saw Gino, Mike, Kate, and Mia interspersed between the guests, but it wasn't any of them. Then a slim brunette woman with pulled, slicked back hair stood up. She was wearing a stunning navy off-the-shoulder full-length dress with heels to match. A wave of jasmine hit me as she stood up right next to me.

In a hushed voice, I said, "Sara, is that you? You look amazing."

She smiled back and batted her eyes, making the smoldering eye shadow come into full effect. "Gee, thanks, Leo. You clean up pretty good yourself." She leaned in closer. "Franco's here. He's in the back."

The effect of her appearance immediately faded when she said that name.

Standing tall and surveying the church, I found him sitting in the back row with three other men. His bright blue eyes were scanning the room. It's as though he knew someone was watching him, and he met my gaze and nodded, tipping his hand to his head. I had to fight off the feeling of hate that was building. This was time for Sal.

I took in a deep breath and leaned down to Sara's ear. "I just spoke to John. Seems like Sal did update his will and some documents for Sigaros. He said Sal never had a partner and that the papers were with Sal when he left John's office on Monday. The documents have to be in Sal's bookshelf."

Sara looked up at me bright-eyed. "We have to get back in there as soon as possible."

I looked straight at her, and in a steeled voice, said, "You do not go in there until we clear things up. Franco is too dangerous and he's having all of us watched. There's too much risk. I don't want anything to happen to you. Is that clear?"

She took a step back, seeing how set I was, and just looked at me a moment. "Okay, Leo. But we need to talk about this more after the service."

I nodded and turned to walk away. Three steps away, I remembered. "Hey, Sara." She was halfway seated and stood back up. Still in a hushed voice, I asked her, "Can you come to dinner at my parents' house Sunday?"

She looked at me a minute and whispered back with a smile, "Sure."

I sat just as Val was approaching the podium.

33

I have no problem talking with people one-on-one or even in a group. I can navigate around conversations, get a read if someone's interested or not, know when to make jokes, or pull back a little. But public speaking to an audience where I know maybe five percent is not within my comfort zone. My palms were clammy as my name was called by Val to come up and talk.

Fumbling in my jacket pocket, I finally got my speech out and shifted through the cards making sure they were in the right order with my late addition to the notes. I'd added a line from one of the books on Sal's shelf that jumped off the page at me.

Val placed a hand over the cards, cupping them together with his other one. "Leo, whatever you say, it'll be good. Just speak from the heart."

The acid that had been building up in my throat faded away a little. Looking out at the crowd, there were people sniffling, those with bowed heads, those looking straight at me, and there was Franco sitting with that same smug grin he had when he showed up to Sigaros with those papers. I wanted so much to smack that grin from his face.

"Thank you all for coming." I looked straight at Franco. "My good friend Sal was one of a kind. True and honorable." I turned and looked out over the crowd. "Every person has a past, and we all come from somewhere. We learn from our past. Father Accardi and Mr. Rossi gave you all a glimpse of that past and Sal's journey. I met Sal a little over half a year ago. Had you told me then that I'd be where I am now, I wouldn't have believed you. But I have Sal to thank for giving me purpose and a kick in the pants to get moving. Sal had a way of knowing a person and fostering what that person needed to motivate themselves into action. I look out now at the faces of people I know, have just met, and don't know. But you're all here for Sal. If you're here, you were likely at one point in time helped by him. A person's actions or rather deeds dictate how they are remembered. I had an opportunity to look at some of Sal's books in his office today and found a page that was flagged and stood out to me, and I think it will to all of you.

'It is the action, not the fruit of the action, that is important. You have to do the right thing. It may not be in your power, it may not be in your time, that there will be any fruit. But that doesn't mean you stop doing the right thing. You may never know what results come from your action, but if you do nothing, there will be no result.'

This showing of people—his friends, his community, and his family—speaks to the goodness of Salvatore Accardi and his desire to do the right thing, no matter the results. His memory will live on with us. Thank you."

A sense of relief immediately washed over me as I sat back down and just let myself listen to the last homily. The service ended with a procession outside with Sal's body headed to the hearse. I saw Mike, Mia, and Kate further down the procession, and Mia turned back, found me, and with tears, smiled at me.

I attempted to navigate through the crowd to catch up with them, but someone held my arm back and tugged me out of the procession. "Leo, you need to know something."

I looked down to see a well-dressed, thinning, white-haired man with a slight hunch. "Angelo, glad you made it."

He grinned. "Wouldn't miss it." Motioning with his head to the front of the church where Franco stood, he said, "Especially with him back in town. He's already advertising that he's back to collect on the loans Sal put up with interest. He was just talking with that lady of yours in the beautiful blue dress. She left in quite a hurry, and I saw his three goons trail her. They will not go easy on her if she's got something they want. You'd better go check on her."

My stomach sank, and the back of my hair started to stand on end. *Sara's headed back to Sigaros to check the bookshelf.* I took off, trying to find any signs of her. Nothing. Weaving my way through the crowd of people, I made my way to the doors of the church. With my height and the few steps leading up to the church, it gave me a good vantage point. Still nothing. I did see Detective Thomas, and he was walking right to me. *This is not the time, detective.*

Sure enough, the detective wanted to talk to me. "Leo, nice speech. I don't agree with everything you said, but it was still nice."

Without stopping, I continued past him gritting my teeth.

The detective continued. "Just to let you know, we've closed the case."

That stopped me in my tracks. I turned still with clenched teeth and said, "Oh really, you got the guy who killed Sal then?"

He scratched the back of his head. "Well, not exactly. We have a drug addict with a gun matching the ballistics we pulled from the body."

"What! A drug addict broke in, fought with Sal, then pulled a gun and shot him in the back and then the chest, and didn't take anything?"

With hands in his pocket, the detective said, "The addict was allegedly in the area at the time of the killing and has a known history of aggravated assault."

I just shook my head and left. Running to Sal's car, I jumped in, turned the engine over and, trying not to hit anyone with the boat on wheels, I lurched forward as I placed it into drive and squealed around the first corner. I almost slammed right into the third car in the funeral procession.

My phone buzzed. It was a text from Sara. *I'm going back to Sigaros while Franco's busy at the funeral. We need to see if Sal left those documents in the book. I'll let you know what I find.* I immediately called her. No answer.

Out loud, I said, "Oh sure, but I have to answer your call."

There was an opening in the procession. I tossed the phone down on the seat and slammed on the gas pedal. I weaved through the surrounding neighborhood to avoid the procession to the cemetery. I was ten minutes away from Sigaros.

My phone rang. "Sara! What are you doing?"

"Quiet! I'm here looking at the books. Didn't you get my message? You weren't the only one with a spare key. Never mind, I found some of the documents. I haven't had—"

In a hurried and hushed voice, I asked, "Sara, Sara, Sara? What's going on?"

In a hushed voice, she said, "Someone's coming in the front door. What should I do?"

My heart sank. I was still five minutes away. In as calm a voice as I could, I said, "Hide. Find someplace in the office and hide. Don't make a sound. If anyone does find you, just give them what they want. I'm on my way." She hung up.

Please let it be that Taser-happy security guard.

I messaged Gino telling him that Sara may be in trouble and to head over to Sigaros.

I pulled up to the side of the plaza and crept around the side of the building, checking to see if anyone was out front. Deserted. I hurried to the front door.

Gently turning the door handle, it was unlocked. I could hear the faint scuffling of a chair and tape being opened. Slinking in through the door, I hear a muffled cry followed by a loud thwack. It was coming from the office. I hurried as quietly as I could through the lounge to the door of the office. Peeking through the slightly opened door, I saw the three of Franco's men standing over Sara. She was seated, taped to the chair. A small cut with a crimson line of blood was showing above her left cheek and was starting to trickle.

The enforcer, Daniel, who'd been with Franco earlier, began barking out orders. "Sam, keep searching the room. Mr. Verga wants that book. Michael, keep her from moving."

The one standing behind Sara held her shoulders down.

Daniel continued and, with a sneer, said, "Now I'm going to ask one more time nicely, and if I don't like the answer, then we get to play a little. Where's the book Sal kept all his loans in?"

Sara stared right back at him shaking her head. He slapped her across the face over the same crimson line, creating a smeared, bloodied line that spread down her face. I turned back to the lounge and picked up a heavy brass ashtray off the table, and rushed through the door. In the time it took for me to grab the ashtray and rush in, the one standing in front of Sara had pulled out a sizable knife and was approaching her wide-eyed face. The one behind her was holding her head still as she thrashed.

They hadn't seen me come in and clearly weren't ready. I let loose the ashtray and knocked Daniel across the temple. He dropped to the ground. The one behind Sara let go of her head and was circling around. Sara let loose a hard kick to one side of the man's knee who'd been holding her down, giving me an opening to go after the other guy barreling down on me. He was quick but not used to anything other than boxing, it seemed. I dodged a few punches and took a roundhouse to the ribs that made my whole chest scream. I pulled him in closer, wrapping him in a choke taking him down to the floor as he thrashed and felt him gradually go limp as I set him on the ground.

The one who got his knee kicked in stood up, clutching his leg, and slapped Sara hard enough to knock the chair over. She didn't move.

I stood up tall and squared off. The man was limping. I took three good shots to the torso. My chest screamed again. Off balance, I took an upper cut and a roundhouse dropping to my knee. I threw all my weight at the man's hurt knee. He fell to the ground and I gained position on top and let loose with one, two, three, four heavy slams to the head. All the frustration from the last few days seemed to rush through my arms with each blow.

I vaguely heard a shout from behind me. It was Gino, and he'd brought Mike with him. I slammed another hit to the man's face and another. I felt their arms pulling me off. I stood, almost lifting both of them off the ground with me.

With a plea in his voice, Gino yelled, "It's us, Leo!"

Mike followed by saying, "Stop! Sara needs help."

I stopped. Looking over, I saw she was unconscious. I went over and checked her head. She had a large welt where the goon had slapped her and where she had hit the ground. Mike and Gino untied her arms as I lifted her to the ground.

Panting, I said, "Mike, call 911. We need an ambulance."

I checked her pulse and breath. They were regular. I turned to the men on the floor, who weren't moving. Gino had checked to make sure they were alive.

"Gino, stay with her."

I scrambled up the ladder and grabbed the book *Common Sense*. There were the papers. I shoved them in my suit jacket and hurried back to Sara.

The medics arrived, looking over the scene. I'd taken Sara out of the office to the lounge, and the medics took her. I got into the ambulance with her just as the police were arriving.

34

In the ED, the doctor and nurses took over from the EMTs and started caring for Sara, and sent me out of the room.

Waiting to know how she was doing was nerve-racking. I was about to burst into the ED when after thirty minutes, a nurse came out saying Sara was stable and talking, followed by the ED doctor saying she'd need to stay overnight. A small wave of relief hit me, finally knowing she was okay, and I sat back in that hard plastic chair that all hospital waiting rooms seem to have and placed my hands over my face.

It must have only been five minutes when I heard the voice of a nurse pointing someone in my direction. The adrenaline that was charging through my system just a little while ago was fading, and the weariness was setting in. My arms and legs felt disconnected. I looked down at my hands to see my knuckles were bloodied, but I didn't feel any pain. I looked back up to see Detective Thomas approach me with Franco behind him and another enforcer, but not one of the ones I'd just pummeled.

Detective Thomas had a furrowed brow and stood over me, looking down. "Leo! What the hell were you doing at Sigaros? Did you beat the hell out of all those guys? I told you specifically that Sigaros is Mr. Verga's now. Any entry is considered illegal and what you did to those men constitutes multiple counts of assault. What do you have to say?"

I sat straight up in my chair. I pulled back my ponytail and brushed my beard down and stood straight up, a full head above the detective, and just looked down at him. He didn't lose my gaze or back away.

Franco interjected. "Now, Detective Thomas, there's no need for all that. I'm sure Leo and I can come to an understanding."

With an open hand, Franco motioned for me to walk with him down a side corridor. Alone in the hallway, he leaned back with his hands in his pockets. I stood in the middle, looking straight at him.

In that same greasy raspy voice, he spoke. "Shame things like this happening to your friend. But they do happen and to all kinds of people. I need to spell this out for you so that it's clear."

He stood up and looked straight at me with his piercing eyes. His voice was a little more graveled. "Sigaros is mine. Sal's legacy will be nothing. I told Sal I'd make him pay. I want Sal's book of loans, or your girlfriend gets charged with breaking and entering and you with assault. Not to mention what else may happen to her or your brother if I don't get what I want."

He smiled, turning away, walking back to the detective and the new enforcer. "I want the book by tomorrow. If you give it to me, you won't ever see me again, and since I'm so generous, I'll forget any collection of debt that Sara may owe if it's in Sal's books. Come on, Vincente, let's go."

I just watched him go. I wanted to tear him apart.

Vincente was as tall as me and dressed in dark jeans and a black T-shirt. He looked to be more my age with olive skin and thick black hair.

I heard Vincente lean in and speak to Franco in a hushed voice. "We never talked about doing things this way. It's not right what happened to the girl." Franco just looked straight through him for a moment and continued walking.

I turned and faced Franco's back and, in a steeled voice, said, "I'll get you the book."

Without turning, Franco said, "Good." He placed a card with a number on the table next to the waiting room chairs. He turned to the detective. "Come on, R. J. Let's talk."

35

I've never enjoyed hospital waiting rooms. With my parents working as administrators, I inevitably wound up coming to hospitals when I was younger, waiting for them to finish up some work.

I hated seeing the different people anxiously sitting there for news of their loved ones and the angst I saw on their faces knowing something bad had happened. Being on the other side of it was just what I expected. Constant waiting and thoughts racing trying to make sure you don't miss an update or even dreading the update. The ray of good news came from that first meeting with the doctor, letting me know Sara was okay. The nurses were great about letting me know what was going on every few hours. I'd let Gino, Mike, Kate, and Mia know what was going on with Sara, and I filled Gino in on what Franco was after.

With Franco's threat, I wasn't about to leave Sara here alone. So I sat and waited and thought about what to do.

At about five in the morning, with a cup of coffee in his hand, Gino walked in. "Leo, go home. I'll keep an eye."

I didn't want to leave, but I was dead on my feet, and the soreness from the recent fight was setting in.

Taking the coffee, I asked, "Gino, what am I going to do? I have to give Franco that book. But if I do, he'll use it to make everyone's life miserable. If I don't, he made it clear what would happen to Sara."

Gino sat next to me. "You know if Sal was here, he'd know what to do. Give him the book, Leo. He's not going to stop."

I nodded. "I'm going home. Let me know if there's any changes."

Getting in the Lincoln, my thoughts were still at the hospital, and as I drove, they drifted to all the different scenarios where I didn't give Franco the book, and all hell breaking loose. *What would Sal do?* The cemetery where Sal was laid to rest was just a few blocks from the hospital, and I turned the corner. I figured, why not go ask Sal?

The morning was bitter cold. November in the desert can be bone-chilling. The cemetery opened at six, and a guard told me about the number of funerals from yesterday, and I decided to take my chances on the one in the mausoleum. Sure enough, it was. It was peaceful and plain, with Sal's name in gold leaf on a white marbled tile.

"Sal, what am I going to do? I don't want to go back to one of my other get-rich-quick-and-easy attempts. I was just getting to like the idea of running Sigaros. How'd you get Franco to leave last time? I can't give him that book of yours to use to try and collect money from everyone and let him use Sigaros as his base. How'd he even know about the book, and why'd he come back now? He seems to know all the next steps I've made and is there waiting for me. I wish you were here."

There was a small marble bench just three sections down, and I sat. I stayed there thinking for another ten minutes when an older woman approached with a handful of flowers. She was slow in her pace and shuffled as she walked, but she stopped at Sal's grave and placed the flowers on the ground next to the others. I noticed her smile and pat the stone slab.

She turned to me. "I see you came to talk to your friend."

I stood up, fixing my ponytail and shirt. "Yes. He always knew the right thing to do, and I came to ask for his advice."

She shuffled over and took the seat I offered, and motioned for me to sit next to her.

"Mr. Accardi was a good man, like you said in your eulogy yesterday. He was a man who tried to do the right thing. I think that's the important thing. Whatever you're needing help with, son, the answer is, 'Do the right thing. If you do nothing, there will be nothing no matter the results.'"

I smiled. "Yeah, I think he'd say that too."

"Mr. Accardi never tried to stop doing what was right, especially if he made a mistake. He did right by me and my children after my husband was killed on a job he was helping out on a long time ago. He never stopped looking for Roland's boy, even after these thirty-odd years. He mentioned he just found him too."

Remembering Sal's book, I turned in my seat to face her. "Wait, are you Mrs. Meryl Jackson? Sal found the kid of Roland Smith?"

"Yes, I'm Mrs. Jackson. Sal had helped me through the years, and I told him and Mr. Rossi years ago to stop sending me anymore. My children are all grown, and I'm well off enough to manage. But he said no, he was going to help as long as he could, that he owed whatever he could to Jackson. When I spoke to him last week, he said he'd spoken to R. J."

"Did he mention anything of where R. J. Smith might be?"

She smiled and lightly slapped my knee. "Now, I told Mr. Accardi the same thing. Roland Junior didn't have his father's last name. His poor mother died in childbirth, and they hadn't been married. R. J. had his mother's name, Thomas. Mr. Accardi found out his mother's family took him back to Cleveland after finding he was placed in foster care. I guess the young man had come back to Vegas a few years ago, and Mr. Accardi just spoke to him to start letting him know what happened and patch things up. Sounded like everything was falling into place."

I turned to look at Sal's grave. My mind was racing. It has to be. R. J. Thomas is Detective Thomas. Sal must have found him and went to talk to him last week and let him know what happened all those years ago. He must have settled things with Detective Thomas. Maybe that's why he was so insistent on Sal's past coming back. He'd just been told what happened. If I can get the detective to be there when I give Franco Sal's book, he can arrest Franco for Sal's murder with probable cause.

I leaned back against the cold marbled wall and heard a crinkle in my jacket. I had Sal's documents. I had completely forgotten about them while at the hospital. The first one was titled Business Agreement. I flipped through what seemed to be endless paragraphs of legal jargon. Finally, one section caught my eye regarding business partners. It clearly stated, "Mr. Salvatore Accardi is the sole proprietor without partner. In the event of the death of the owner, the manager of Sigaros is tasked with running the day-to-day operations outlined in the owner's will with the proceeds to be handled between Mr. Lugino Rossi and Father Valentino Accardi."

I stopped and looked back at the mausoleum. "Thanks, Sal. That's all I need."

I didn't bother looking at the will. I shoved both papers back in my suit jacket and took out my phone.

I stood up and faced Mrs. Smith. "Thank you so much. I think I know what to do next." I touched her hand, and she smiled back, and I rushed out to the Lincoln.

264

36

R eaching the car, I called Val. "Hey, Val. I need to drop off some papers Sal left in his office to John for safe keeping. Can you let him know I'm coming?"

"Sure, thing, son. What's going on? You seem a little off."

I was a little off. The idea of trying to pin a murder on a gangster was setting in and it wasn't going to be easy. In as calm a voice as I could muster, I said, "Just tired and I went to see Sal's mausoleum."

With a catch in his throat, he said, "It's hard on all of us. Go slow and take care of yourself. I'll let John know."

I took in a deep breath. "Thanks, Val."

For my plan to get Franco arrested, I need Detective Thomas' help.

I finally got a hold of Gino on the second try. "How's Sara doing?"

In a sleepy voice, he said, "She's good. Nurse said she's fine."

"I need your help. I need you to get me information on two people. The first one is Detective Thomas."

"Wait, what?"

"It seems as though Detective Thomas may be the son of one of the caddies that was killed in the bank job, and I need to make sure."

"How'd you figure this out?"

"I just spoke with Mrs. Jackson, and she let me in on the fact that Sal figured out that the detective may be Roland Junior, the son of the caddie Roland Smith."

There was a pause on the other line, and in a low voice, Gino said, "Why the hell didn't Sal tell me about this? Okay, I'll look into it. Who's the other one?"

"Check on a muscle for hire named Vincente from L.A. He's working with Franco."

"I'll give Angelo a call. He knows more people from there. I'll let you know what I find. What are you up to?"

"I have an idea of how to get Franco arrested. He as much said it to me at the hospital that he came back to take Sigaros and Sal's books by any means. If I can prove he had probable cause, then he can be arrested. I'll need the help of the detective to bring Franco in when I meet with him at the office. With the new security system in place, I'll have it all recorded."

"Listen, Leo, this is a bad idea. Franco isn't going to let slip anything that he's done especially if he thinks anything is being recorded. My advice is to give him whatever he wants and protect yourself and any loved ones. I know you're trying to do right by Sal, but he wouldn't want you dead. Don't do this."

"Sal won't get any justice until Franco is arrested. The only way to do this is to give Franco what he wants, and it's all at Sigaros. Franco doesn't know about the new system. This is the only way it'll work. Please, I'm trying to save Sigaros, help the people working there, stop Sal's killer from doing worse, and... most importantly, it's the right thing to do, and there isn't time to do anything else, Gino."

There was a brief pause. "You sound like him, you know that? Sal's given this speech before." Gino paused again. "It really matters this much to you?"

"It's important."

"Okay, I'll get you the info. Be careful, Leo."

"Thanks." I hung up.

37

I dropped off the documents at John's, and by the time I got home, it was already ten. The morning hadn't gotten any warmer. Seems as though the bite of the desert winter was here to stay.

Getting out of the shower, my muscles were stiff, and as my phone rang, I had to shuffle over to it. It was Gino.

Almost like a war correspondent, Gino gave me his report. "Angelo found out that Franco has been recruiting some muscle from L.A.—cashing in on old debts he's collected. The three guys you beat the hell out of were enforcers from low-level crews. Apparently, this guy Vincente isn't from any of the families from Los Angeles. He's known there, he keeps it clean, and he's very good at collecting. Franco apparently has something on his brothers back in Cleveland, and the debt was taken over by Vincente. Franco is having three new enforcers arrive tomorrow."

"I can't wait for those guys to show up." I immediately thought what Franco might do if he had more muscle in town and what he'd try to do to Sara or anyone else. "How's Sara?"

"She's fine. Richie is keeping an eye. He knows what to look for."

"Any word on the detective? Is he connected at all to the caddie Roland Smith from here in Vegas?"

"Looks like he is. But I couldn't find if Sal had spoken to him or not."

With a sigh, I said, "Thanks, Gino. I'm going to call Franco to set up a meet at Sigaros."

"Wait, Leo. I got word from Angelo that Franco has been in contact with someone here in Vegas. They've been feeding him info on Sal, Sigaros, and you. Sounds like it's someone Franco knew in Cleveland. With no head of the family back home, Franco isn't being held accountable to anyone. He's operating alone. Anything he does now he can claim as his, which would allow him to stay."

The information sat in my stomach like lead. I need to move things along and get the detective to help arrest Franco. It needs to be today.

"Thanks, Gino. I'll let you know how it turns out."

"Good luck, kid."

I rang Detective Thomas. Finally, after several desk clerks, I got through. "Hello, Detective Thomas. I have a way to get probable cause on Franco Verga for the murder of Sal, and I need your help to arrest him."

In a dry voice, he said, "Leo, I already told you if it's anything related to Mr. Accardi's murder, we have someone that fits. Let the legal system handle the next steps. It's done."

"I know that Sal came to see you last week. I know it was about how your father died and clearing up what happened. I need you to help me continue what Sal was trying to do."

There was a long pause. "And what was it he was trying to do?"

"The right thing." The line was silent again. "Franco is trying to start up here in town. He's the one who got your father killed."

"Wait, Franco was the one responsible for my father's death?" His voice seemed almost rushed.

"Yes, when Sal met with you, I'm sure he explained what happened. Sal had planned how to get into the bank, but it was Franco that checked the place out and told your father and the other man to go in, knowing there were armed guards."

In a somewhat shaky voice, Detective Thomas said, "Sal said he felt responsible."

There was silence.

"Sal was trying to do the right thing. In a way, he was, but he didn't send your father in to die. Franco was the one."

The detective stammered. "I-I thought he said he was responsible for it."

I continued on. "Franco's the one who killed Sal to get to his books and to all the people he helped over the years. He's trying to start a loan shark operation in town. The book even shows that Sal's been trying to find you over the years to pay back for what happened to your father. I have a way to prove it."

Now in a more even voice, the detective said, "So I'm in that book of his too?"

"Yes, and the book is what Franco wants. If I can show you that book and have you there wouldn't that be enough probable cause to show Franco was planning to take Sigaros and at least start the process to prove Franco killed Sal? It'd be enough to stop Franco and arrest him."

"It would give probable cause." The detective paused again. "What do you need?"

"I need you to be at Sigaros before I meet Franco and be in the humidor across from the office, listening in. I'll also be recording the whole thing. Once you hear me give Franco the book, you walk in and arrest him. I'll message you when I have the exact time of the meeting. Arrive before the meeting and listen in on the conversation."

In a dry voice, the detective said, "I'll be there."

I hung up and took a deep breath in. My ribs didn't hurt as much, and my muscles were starting to loosen up again.

I took out the card Franco had left on the hospital side table and picked up my phone. "Franco. Meet at Sigaros in two hours. I'll give you the book."

In that same raspy voice, Franco replied, dripping with smugness. "Good boy, Leo. Two hours." Click.

38

It was just about dusk when I stepped out of the Lincoln in front of Sigaros. The wind had picked up, and the chills went straight through your clothes and seemed to settle in your bones. Franco and Vincente were standing at the door. It didn't seem as though the cold affected them. Franco, in his wool topcoat, buttoned up to his neck, and Vincente, in his leather jacket, stood guard, surveying the plaza.

Franco smiled and said, "You're making the right move. You know, Leo, when this is all done, I could use someone like you to run a few things. You could sit back after a while and enjoy an easy life. You could help Vincente set things up for me here in town. You two would be a formidable team as part of my crew."

I saw Vincente look back at him, a little astonished, and then go back to his surveillance. I looked straight at him and, with a little more steel in my voice than intended, said, "Never."

Franco shrugged. "Where's the book?"

I pointed to the door. "Inside. Sal's office."

Franco shook his head. "It's not there. I had it searched."

This time I smiled and shrugged. "Apparently, your goons, you know, the ones I beat the hell out of, didn't look hard enough."

Vincente didn't react or move.

Franco stepped closer and, in a harsh tone, said, "I have little regard for people who waste my time." He eyed me.

I fought back the urge to tear his head off. I could hardly wait to see him arrested. Through gritted teeth, I said, "It's in a second safe that Sal showed me."

Franco turned sideways and, with an open palm, gestured to the front door handing me the keys. Sigaros always felt warm when I'd been there, but today the chill had crept into the lounge. I hugged my jacket close to my body.

After we were inside, Vincente spoke up in a stern but controlled voice. "Wait." He walked over. Looking at me, he raised his eyebrows, and I lifted my arms out to the side. Vincente patted me down and, in the same voice, said, "He's clean."

Franco patted Vincente on the back. I noticed the enforcer pull back and make a small gesture as though he'd been touched by something filthy.

"Vincente, wait here while Leo and I go chat in the office."

Vincente made his way over to the bar and sat on one of the stools, looking toward the front door, keeping watch. Franco pointed a finger at the office, and I led the way. Before crossing into the office, I noticed the door to the humidor was opened a crack. The detective was here. He'd gotten my message.

Sal's office was warmer than the main lounge. The brick fireplace and the smaller room seemed to have kept some of their warmth. I didn't have to pull my suit jacket so close to me.

In a harsher voice, Franco said, "Don't waste my time. I want this book now."

"You'll get it. You'll have all the names and amounts. I know you plan on collecting on the money Sal lent out. I know that's why you killed him or had him killed."

He stopped and casually looked down at a bottle of bourbon on the table and held it in his hands. "You know what, Leo? You shouldn't assume so much. I told you I wanted this book. Sal got me kicked out of this town. He got what he deserved. In a way, I can't say that I wouldn't have done what he did back then, but I'm owed. This town is still ripe for the picking."

He tossed the half-empty bottle up and down in his hands. "I tried to get that book from Sal the easy way when my guys went to see him. I can and will make a lot of money from what Sal set up. All his good little deeds in that book of his will turn into the capital I need to set up here." He stopped tossing the bottle and looked at me. "Without any oversight from anyone!"

He slammed the bottle against the fireplace shattering it into dozens of small pieces.

Vincente appeared at the door immediately. Franco held up a hand, not looking at him. In a gravelly and raspy voice, he yelled, "Now! Give me the book!"

Vincente went back to the lounge.

I held up my hands, not wanting to piss him off further. "It's in the fireplace."

Franco was standing behind the couch in front of the mantel and turned, looking it up and down, with his hands in his coat pockets. He looked back at me and motioned with his head for me to go over. I obliged and walked over slowly. Franco watched me closely. I put my hand on the side of the mantle to open the drawer. From the corner of my eye, I saw Franco take his hand out of his pocket and unbutton the top of his coat with his right hand. His hand stayed at the top of the coat until I pulled out the book. Crossing back over to the couch in front of the desk, I handed Franco the book.

I'd just handed the devil his prize.

Franco took the book and thumbed through it, and with a wolfish grin and a gleam in his eye, he said, "Perfect, this is perfect. Sal has it all here. I can take it all. This town won't hold anything back from me now."

My muscles were tense, and I could feel the butterflies in my stomach start up. "You'll never get away with it. The police will figure out that you killed Sal to get to his book."

Franco looked up from the book and cocked his head sideways, squinting his eyes, and looked at me, questioning my last statement. Just as he did, the office door clicked closed with Detective Thomas locking it with one hand behind him and the other hand holding a gun on Franco.

I didn't realize that I'd been holding my breath for so long and let out a long breath and leaned back on the desk.

The detective addressed Franco in a calm authoritarian voice. "Mr. Verga, it seems as though we may have probable cause to bring you in for the murder of Mr. Salvatore Accardi."

All I could think was that this was finally over. But the next words from Franco made me start to second-guess what exactly was going on.

With a grin, Franco said, "Now, R. J. Is that any way to treat an old friend?"

I'd heard Franco call the detective R. J. before in the hospital.

39

In a dry and even tone, Detective Thomas said, "Mr. Verga, please take your hands out of your pockets." Franco obliged. "It seems as though Leo here has all that you said on a recording, and with what I just heard, it sounds like we need to go to the police station."

Franco smiled and started to laugh, but it came out like gravel with his raspy voice as he looked back and forth between the detective and me.

"You think I didn't know about the cameras and alarm system he just put in?" He scoffed. "The first thing I had my guys do when everyone left yesterday was rip out the alarm system and cameras."

My eyes darted around the room. The books had all been taken down. My heart sank. There were no cameras. I looked toward the office door, and the sensor over the top of the door was undone. I turned, looking down at the desk, and walked around to the chair. Components of three or four door alarms and control panels were laying there, all dismantled.

"I've been doing this for a long time, Leo. You think I'm dumb enough to walk into a place that I think was rigged to have me recorded?"

I glanced over toward the outlet to the left of the office door. I had replaced it with the outlet recording device Gabe's security guy had given me. It hadn't been tampered with. It was still working.

I stopped looking at it and looked back at Detective Thomas, who was still pointing the gun at Franco. "Detective Thomas, how do you know Franco?"

The detective didn't look at me.

Instead, Franco spoke up in a calm and cool voice, looking at me. "Detective Thomas and I have a little history, and old ties die hard." Franco looked at Detective Thomas, who was still holding the gun on him. "Don't they, R. J?"

I saw the detective shift his fingers on the trigger of the gun.

"You see, R. J. ran into a little bit of trouble back in Cleveland when he was younger, and I was fortunate enough to be able to help him out. He did well for himself, joined the air force, and then the Las Vegas Metropolitan Department." Franco smiled. "And now he's Detective Thomas. You see, I'd known his father and knew he was in Cleveland after his death." Franco turned to me and wrinkled his brow. "I felt obligated to help. In return, R. J. has been kind enough to let me know what's been going on with the investigation and what you've been up to, Leo. You see, when Sal came to talk to him, R. J. gave me a call, and I explained how it was all Sal's idea and that Sal was truly responsible for his father's death and for all the struggles he had to go through."

Exasperated, I said, almost shouting, "That's not true. It was your plan. It was you who told his father to go into that bank, knowing it wasn't safe. Gino told me what happened. Sal went to Detective Thomas to clear everything up."

I noticed Detective Thomas' eyes darting sideways to me, then back to Franco, and a little sweat was starting to form at his temples. It was still too cold in here for anyone to be sweating.

Franco raised his hands and cocked his head, looking at the detective. "Well, who you gonna believe?" Franco stepped closer to Detective Thomas. "Besides, the only thing I've truly done is ask for this book. I had nothing to do with Sal's murder." With his cold voice and piercing blue eyes, Franco looked straight through the detective and said, "Killing a person isn't easy, especially your first time."

I noticed the detective become a little pale, but he still had his gun on Franco.

Franco continued in the same calm, harsh voice. "It's a little different being on the other side of the law, isn't it, R. J.?" He paused. "Tough to know who can keep a secret."

The detective lowered his gun.

In a panicked voice, I said, "Detective Thomas? Just... just take him in. It's done." I started to walk out from behind the desk.

Detective Thomas turned sideways so that he could see both Franco and me and quickly said, "Stay where you are, Leo. Sit down and don't move."

He raised the gun and pointed it at me. I stepped back, my jaw open, trying to voice a protest, but nothing would come out. I sat in the desk chair.

The detective moved the gun back and forth between Franco and me. The detective's finger was visibly fidgeting on the trigger.

Franco spoke up. "Now I really don't care what happens here, R. J. It appears the only problem you have here is Leo. I have what I want right here." He held up the book. "What you want to do now is your business."

The room was still for what seemed like an eternity. The detective turned his gun back on me. His eyes weren't darting back and forth between Franco and me; they were fixed on me.

Franco smiled with a toothy grin and, in that smug voice, he said, "I'm going to walk out. I was never here." He tipped his fingers to me. "See ya, Leo."

The detective didn't speak. He just looked at me, and I could see the sweat forming above his brow. Franco was headed to the door with the book in his left hand. *It can't end like this. Franco can't just get away. Even if he didn't kill Sal, he was responsible for everything that happened.* Without thinking, I shot up out of my chair and yelled, "Hey!"

Before I could get out the word "Wait," Franco had spun around and pulled a snub nose revolver from inside his topcoat that must have been in a holster over his chest. A shot rang out, hitting the detective in his chest. The detective's gun flashed twice, followed by a deafening roar, and I felt a razorlike cut across my right shoulder followed by an intense pain, and the lamp on the desk shattered. A force I hadn't seen pushed me back down into the chair. The detective fell to the ground looking at me as he did with wide eyes and an open mouth.

I clutched my right arm. A warm liquid feeling started to spread over my left hand, and I looked over. My shoulder was bleeding. I pressed harder over the wound to stop it, and I grimaced, leaning over the desk looking at Franco.

I could hear Vincente banging on the door and leaning his shoulder into it.

Franco walked over and kicked Detective Thomas' foot. He didn't move. Franco shook his head, looking down at the man he just shot. Then he turned his blue-piercing gaze toward me. He started to raise his gun at me and, with a grin, said, "You know, it's gonna be a lot of fun being—" Before he could finish, there was another loud roar that came from where the detective lay.

Franco's eyes went wide, and his face went pale, clutching his gut. He turned and looked down to face the detective, who was holding a smoking gun up at him. "You rat bastard!"

Franco unloaded his gun into the detective whose body went limp. Franco turned his gun toward me. The gun made a clicking sound, and it made me catch my breath as I leaned on the desk.

Franco threw the gun on the ground and stumbled toward the back of the couch. Vincente burst through the office door, gun in hand, and looked at the dead man on the floor, then at me, and finally at Franco. He came around to the back of the couch.

Franco looked up at him and said, "Kill him and get me to a hospital. I've still got plans, and you still owe me a debt. Don't forget about your brothers."

Vincente turned to me, and I looked up at him and took a deep breath. I leaned back in the desk chair. I fixed my ponytail, squared my shoulders, placed my hands on the armrest, and sat up tall. I held his gaze. He nodded. Raising the gun at me, he winked. He turned quickly and shot Franco in the chest twice.

After the shots, he said, "There's nothing you can do now. There's no more debt."

Franco slumped down to the floor, resting his back against the frame of the couch. Pink foam started to froth at the sides of his mouth with a trickle of bright red blood. He looked up at me, and without moving, I looked down at him.

In a garbled voice, Franco said, "If I see Sal, and I think I will…" He followed it with a blood-filled cough, "… I'll tell him you say hello." His bright blue eyes went dim as his pupils widened, and he slumped over to the floor.

Vincente stood there looking down at Franco. He turned to me. "I'm sorry about Sara. That shouldn't have happened to her… or anyone. You won't see me again."

I nodded. Vincente looked around the room and went through the broken office door.

I sat there. I looked around the room, grabbed my right shoulder, and took a deep breath in. I could hear police sirens in the distance, drawing closer.

40

It was one in the afternoon. I unbolted the outside doors to Sigaros, walked in, and turned on the lights. The place had that musty smell that needed airing out. I walked behind the bar, grabbed the bottle of gin, and made my way to the walk-in humidor. I took a Partagus, walked into Sal's office, turned on the lights, and sat down at the desk.

My body ached. My right arm was out of the sling after a few days, but it still gave me jolts of pain with certain movements. Although it was nothing compared to the feeling of mental exhaustion. It had only been a week since the shooting. The police were satisfied with my story of Franco and Detective Thomas killing each other. I'd left Vincente out of the story.

I called Sara and told her to be in by three.

I went about organizing the papers on the desk. I'd run by Sal's lawyer John earlier in the day and added Sal's will and the business document for Sigaros to the ever-growing pile. Sal's business document and will stipulated under a section called "Acts of Succession" that in the event of his death, Val and Gino would be benefactors and, if they saw fit, they could sell Sigaros as long as that person was in keeping with the business's mission statement. Sal's will was very clear in its statement. I recognized it from a line in a book in his library that I'd started to read. "It's the action, not the fruit of the action, that's important. You have to do the right thing. It may not be in your time that there will be any fruit, but that doesn't mean you stop doing the right thing."

Also, Sal left his Lincoln as a business car to be used as needed.

I put out my cigar and took a pull on my drink. It had been the first moment of quiet over these last few weeks that I could remember. It felt good to be still and have a moment with my thoughts.

I remembered back to that last day that I spoke with Sal. He had left the bar with me. I hadn't realized then all that came with it. It feels like a heavy weight to bear; the responsibility, trust, and reliance of others on myself to do the right thing for them. The people who stood by me over the last few weeks put their faith in my decisions.

I pulled out my book of ideas and placed it on the desk. Looking down at the book, it seemed like a lifetime ago that I'd last opened it. I looked over at the mantle and walked over to the hidden drawer, clicked it open, placed the book in the compartment, and closed it.

By the time I got the desk in order, Sara was walking through the door.

She yelled out from the front of the bar. "Leo? Where are you?"

"I'm in Sal's office," I shouted back and pulled down the rest of my drink.

She walked through the door looking as great as ever in her black leather jacket and skintight black jeans with high-heeled boots. She had poise and determination in her steps, as well as what looked to be sorrow in her face, along with the well-healing scar that was developing from the beating she recently took.

"How you holding up?" I asked her.

"Fake it till you make it," she said.

The look on her face told me not to ask more. She'd been through a lot with Sal's death and the recent hospital stay. She handled it like a champ. Without her, I don't think I would've gotten as far as I did or found the resilience to follow through. I just wish I was here when those thugs showed up. The scar that showed and those that didn't won't be going away anytime soon.

"Getting comfortable?" she asked.

I was squirming in the seat. "The chair doesn't seem right. I can't get settled. It feels too big."

I smelt her jasmine perfume which hit me like a soft wave.

"It'll feel better in time. It's yours now."

"I know. I just..." I paused and put my hands on the sides of my eyes, and leaned all the way back, looking at the ceiling... I wish I knew what Sal had in mind," I said with a deep sigh.

"Hey!" she said, exasperated.

I straightened up and looked at her face. She looked surprised, angry, and was teary-eyed.

"This is it... the place, the people, the history, the culture of Sigaros, you!"

"What?" I said, surprised.

She put her hand on her hips and leaned over the desk. "You're an idiot, Leo... it's his legacy. He wanted to preserve the idea and feeling of what he built. He needs you to do that."

Tears started as she spoke next and sat on the edge of the desk.

"You stood up to Franco, you stood your ground, and didn't back down from those assholes who beat the hell out of me. You confronted the detective. You gave Sal the justice he deserved. Sigaros will open again tomorrow. Most importantly, you kept Sal's values alive."

I stood and crossed from behind the desk to stand in front of her.

"Don't you dare hug me. I'm not broken. I can stand on my own."

In a low and calm voice, I said, "I know you can... it's just now you look like crap, and people are about to show up. I can't have you all runny-nosed."

She looked surprised and a little angry and stifled a cry. I handed her my handkerchief.

She took it begrudgingly and cleaned her eyes, and finally grinned.

I held her shoulders. "Thanks, Sara."

"You're welcome. What now?" she asked.

I moved back to the desk and sat down. "There's lots to do. The twins will be in soon to help clean up. Distributors and a new security vendor will be arriving first thing tomorrow. Gabe is coming to go over to see about expanding the place. The bar needs to be made up and restocked, and we have new bartenders arriving for training. The bar is now your responsibility. I expect an update by tonight for anything needed for tomorrow's opening."

Sara just looked at me and didn't say anything.

I looked up at her. "What?"

"Look at you being all responsible and ambitious."

I grinned. "Get to work."

She said, "Yes, boss" with a smile, turned, and started to walk out of the office.

I stopped her at the door. "Oh, do you think you could make dinner this Sunday at my parents' house?"

She stopped and put her hand on the door. Still smiling, she said, "Sure. But you know, it's not good for the boss to be trying to go out with an employee."

I stumbled over my next few words. "Well... umm... if you don't feel comfortable. I totally understand..."

She laughed a little. "I'll be there. Good thing I'm almost done with my law classes and studying for the bar. I won't be an employee for much longer."

I smiled back at her. "That is a good thing."

Just then, the twins poked their heads behind Sara, giggling, and she immediately started barking orders.

I stood and went to the new safe I'd purchased. I took a legal-sized paper out of my pocket, opened it, and had to reread the title. "Deed of Trust: Sigaros." It had my name signed and printed in the ownership box. I slipped the piece of paper into the safe next to a thumb drive labeled "Recording" and closed it. Gino and Angelo, along with Val, had helped me with the business loan.

I sat back down at the desk. I opened the top drawer to start going through the mail and signing checks. I saw Sal's lighter there in the desk. I took it out and put it in the safe. I went back to the desk and put my lighter and keys to the Lincoln in the top drawer.

I hadn't been much for staying in one place, but it seems as though that's changed. This is home. It's my responsibility to continue to help Sigaros and the people in it. Do the right thing. If you do nothing, there will be nothing, no matter the results.

Mike called out from in front of the bar. "Leo! Call for you. Said it's an old friend."